Redrowen Vol. 2

Wolf

D. C. Hart

ISBN: 978-1-7366643-2-2 (Paperback)

Any references to historical events, real people, or real places are used fictitiously. Names, characters, and places are products of the author's imagination. Any resemblance to any actual persons, living or dead, organizations, events or locales is entirely coincidental.

Cover images by Muazz Shaail.

Volume 2
First edition, Third printing 2021

To every wonderful person who has supported me on this fantastic adventure, I could not have done any of this without each and every one of you. From the family I was born with, to the family I have found along the way, this series is as much for you as it is for me. Never forget who you are inside and know that you are never alone. May the world I have created inspire you to find wonder in your own lives.

A special thanks to the Brutal Force and Rukus Gaming families for all the support you have provided throughout this journey so far. Though I am just getting started, I could not have come this far without you.

Thank you to my amazing cover designer (Shaail) for being there as I learn step by step the ins and outs of what it means not just to write a book, but to publish one.

And to my hotel family, you are missed. Never will I forget the long hours, the early mornings, and the late nights with each and every one of you.

One

Hearing her voice is like hearing the collective voices of the gods themselves. Even when filled with worry and despair, Esse's voice is a beacon of hope in an otherwise dismal world.

I thought I was a goner for a moment there. If I am dead, then I am most certainly in hell. My whole body is on fire.

I can hear Esse's steady heartbeat, like a tiny drum, beside me and feel her hand on mine but I still lack the strength to speak to her. Once strong enough to finally speak, I cannot help myself.

"At least you didn't eat my heart, little fairy."

I can tell before she has had time to react that Esse is masterfully resisting the urge to strike me. Ironically, and unbeknownst to her, my comment is at least partially genuine.

"That is the first thing you say to me after nearly dying!" Esse's voice is filled with an understandable mix of relief and irritation with a thinly veiled layer of anger.

I love riling her up. I think I would have missed her dramatic reactions to my antics should I have died, assuming a dead lycanthrope can miss things.

Still afraid to open my eyes for fear that I am dreaming, I blindly reach a hand up towards her face, every flawless feature of that beautiful fairy face tells me that it is her, including the tears on her cheeks. I gently brush her tears aside as I explain myself.

"I wasn't joking my little fairy. In lycanthrope culture, we eat the hearts of our dying or recently deceased loved ones to keep their spirits with us."

I let my eyes flutter open, taking in the sight of Ellesse's storm-cloud eyes and flawless features, framed in messy silver curls.

"That is awful, but kind of sweet. Does it work?" She questions timidly.

In truth, I do not know if the tradition of consuming a fallen lycan's heart works or not, though it probably would have helped my mother had she been afforded the opportunity to properly grieve and lay to rest my father. Losing him killed her in the end. To think, the same could have happened to me today...

"I am glad to say I'm not sure. By the way, do not think I am just letting you off the hook for being so damn reckless when you promised me that you would run. Honestly Esse what were you thinking?" I scold her, genuinely distraught at the multitude of ways this situation could have ended horribly.

The last thing I remember before everything went black was Ellesse being carried into the sky by Chiron, her second, while I struggled to fend off a member of the Order amidst a wildfire created by one of Esse's freak lightning storms.

So, a typical Tuesday.

"I know," Ellesse mumbles sheepishly. "In my defense, I was poisoned with an arrow. Running was not an option." She adds quickly.

I stop her before she can pout her way out of a well-deserved lecture.

"And what should you have done to avoid that arrow?" I growl accusingly.

"Run away," she grumbles, worming her way into the line of my chest in an adorable attempt to appease my judgmental mood.

"Being cute will not save you," I inform her.

Ellesse can be so stubborn sometimes. Granted, she is an extremely powerful guardian to a divine relic, known as the Fountain of Divine Life, so she is no ordinary fairy. However, none of that

2

changes the reality that losing my Esse would destroy me, leaving me with no will to live.

Esse continues her attempts to weasel her way out of a lecture with her charm, nosing her way into the center of my chest and curling her knees in toward her stomach to form a tiny ball on top of my rib cage.

How utterly unfair. I think in bitter admiration.

She is quite skilled. Kiro, my wolf, points out.

Esse has all the charm and beauty of a twenty-year-old with all the wisdom of her nine centuries of life, making her ideally suited for the task of manipulating me into feeling sorry for attempting to protect her. Despite her special skills of manipulation, I am determined to make her see the error of her reckless behavior.

"Well, what about you, grumpy wolf." She counters softly. "You almost broke both your promises to me."

She has you there. Kiro points out, finally having calmed himself after our near-death experience.

She is right. I admit to Kiro. *If I had died, even to save her, I would have failed to keep my promise to her. Perhaps I can make it up to her by keeping that promise right now.*

"You know full well I did not have a choice. But you are right. What if I make it up to you? Seeing as the forest is...well you know, why don't you come and live with us in Ireland? You could bring that stone that you are so desperate to kill yourself for, and there is plenty of sparse, privately owned forest for Chiron to hide in. A friend of mine owns several dozen acres of woodland and open fields. You could hide the stone there, and I could keep my promise and show you the world outside, just until this forest grows back."

A tense, thoughtful silence falls over Ellesse at the mention of the keystone. I worry, for a moment, that her precious stone might have been lost or damaged in the conflict with the Order.

"Spill it, little fairy. What has shut you up so suddenly? It isn't like you not to jump at the thought of taking an adventure with me."

More than anything, I need her to come with me now. Though I still do not understand how everything works with regards to the keystone and the fountain, I know that Ellesse is the guardian of both. I also know that as the guardian, she must remain close to the keystone at all times to protect it, though she must never use it. Using the keystone would ultimately kill her by draining her of life energy, known to the faeries as ani.

Something we can never allow. Kiro points out.

Agreed. If protecting this stone means so much to her that she would risk her life for it, then the best thing we can do now is to keep the damned object as close as possible...

"Kal...Kal...Kal!"

My eyes snap open, taking in the sight of the most precious thing in my entire world; *Ellesse*.

Looking down at me now, with the most brilliant silvery blue eyes, is my precious, wingless fairy guardian. A characteristically warm smile graces her flawless, porcelain face, and her curly silver hair catches lightly on the midday breeze, fluttering lightly across her neck and chin. She reaches to pull back the loose strands and tuck them carefully behind her pointed ears.

I must have fallen asleep in her lap again. Please tell me I did not drool this time...

"You must have been dreaming of something rather intense." She beams down at me, her voice brimming with amusement. "You were quite...expressive." She glances away, her cheeks burning a familiar shade of rosy red; a shade that I have become extremely fond of.

"I suppose you could say that...I was dreaming of you." I inform her, half intending to rile her up further.

"You always say that." Esse puffs out her lip in an all too familiar pout.

Six months have come to pass since her forest burnt to the ground, forcing Esse to live with me, and still, her pout gets to me every time. I reminisce dreamily.

Soft. Kiro criticizes pointedly.

Yes, I know, you think she makes me too soft. Since when is soft a bad thing? We are fighting for the right of every lycan to be as soft or as warrior-like as they choose. I remind my judgmental wolf.

"I speak only the truth," I assure Esse. Without thinking, my right hand travels to the center of my chest, perhaps reliving the events of that day six months ago.

To save my life, Ellesse broke one of the oldest laws of her people and embedded the keystone to the legendary fountain within my chest. I cannot imagine the courage her decision must have taken. She was not sure that she had the strength to accomplish such a task, yet she attempted it anyway. Esse risked unleashing the power of a small sun for the sole purpose of saving my life.

I smile to myself upon realizing that, had her efforts failed, Esse would have been left guarding my corpse for eternity. I dare not bring that up to her though. Bringing such topics up to Esse, even as a joke, is the fastest way to get yourself struck by lightning or sucked into a tornado.

Before either of us can say more, a familiar set of silent footsteps approaches. Judging by the tension brought with them, my day off has just come to an end.

I suppose I should not be surprised. After all, I am only attempting to completely alter the laws and traditions of my entire species. Some complications are to be expected.

"Oh, hello Red!" Ellesse greets the silent, russet-red-haired handyman with the same cheerful tone that brightens the day of each member of our odd family.

There is something to be admired in the way Esse remains cheerful despite the tragic nature of her past. Even now, despite Red's interruption of my only day off with her, Esse smiles the same genuine smile. Most faeries would have mourned themselves to death over the collective loss of their home, their life's purpose, and half their remaining power, but not Esse; she bounced back only failing to smile in the days that followed the passing of her beloved nighthound, Bartro.

Bartro was killed protecting the Northern Forest, his home, against a heinous attempt by the Order to siphon the power of the Fountain of Divine Life. He fought bravely and with his last efforts opened a tunnel so that we could retrieve Ellesse from where she was hidden. Grievously injured and poisoned with insecticides, Esse would not have lived had Bartro not dug her out of her hiding place. Even Kiro still mourns the loss of the jovial nighthound, having considered the beast a friend.

Red smiles apologetically at Esse, addressing her rather than me. "I need to borrow him. I am sorry."

"No need to apologize Red. You are just the messenger, I am sure." She sighs, turning to me with a "you owe me" look on her face.

"Another time," Esse states pointedly, which is her non-negotiable means of telling me not to let this happen again. And yes, I will be forced to make this up to her later if I wish to avoid sleeping under a literal storm cloud.

I suppose I already owe her my life, what is one more debt on top of that?

With a groan of resistance, I turn toward Red knowing that he will say nothing more without being prompted. Red is not an anti-social or inhospitable man, he is simply a man of few words. Like the rest of our tiny band of rouges, Red has lost a great deal and, even now, carries his pain and loss with him like a heavy set of chains.

"So, what problem have you brought me today Red?" I ask him with a burdened sigh.

Lazy. Kiro remarks.

Not the time Kiro.

"It's your sister," Red informs me.

"Okay Red, you cannot just say things like that without context. Your statement could mean anything from: your sister is dying, to your sister is yelling at me and I do not want to deal with it. Is Sela safe?" I can already feel a headache brewing in my temples.

"She is fine. But she is yelling. You had better call her."

I release a sigh of relief and exasperation.

At least she is not hurt.

"Thank you, Red, I will just be another minute."

Red offers a nod then turns to make his way back to the house with one last apologetic glance toward Esse, whom he views as the undisputed right hand of this unconventional pack. We watch him leave in frustrated silence before turning our attention back to what we were doing.

"Esse, I am so sorry. I know I promised you no work today, but it is Sela…" I begin begging for mercy but Esse shakes her head, interrupting me by promptly leaning forward to kiss my forehead, a gesture that has become much more casual for her of late. The boldness of her gesture leaves me temporarily stunned, like a goldfish whose bowl has been shaken.

"I never assumed that keeping you safe while you attempt to rewrite the traditions of your species and unite the primes would be easy. Go, help your sister, and tell her I cannot wait for her holiday visit."

How could I have forgotten the Fall Moon Feast? With less than a month to go before Esse's first Fall Moon Feast with the family, and with Sela's pack flying in for it, I really will not have many more days off. I realize.

For the last month, I have spent most of my free time preparing for the yearly event in an attempt to make the celebration fairy-friendly for Esse. Traditionally, the Fall Moon Feast, a festival adopted from the Viking tradition of honoring the final harvest before winter, is filled with exhibitions of strength and combat

7

prowess. Being a peaceful species, faeries like Esse derive little pleasure from fighting, even if no one is harmed. Therefore, this year's festival will contain games and tests of strength that do not rely solely upon combat. Esse has even taken to planning part of the festivities.

I wonder what I would be doing right now had I not wandered into her forest half a year ago. Esse has always had a way of knowing exactly what to say and do even in situations with which she has had little experience. She is certainly not like any lycanthrope female that I have met.

"I promise I will make this up to you later," I assure Esse as I reluctantly rise from her lap to make my way back to the house to call Sela.

The manor grounds are vast and well kept, sprinkled with shrubbery and young Ash and Oak trees which line the many walkways of the forty-five-acre property. Two water sources, located on the central grounds and hunting grounds of the property, are well stocked with fish and seasonal waterfowl. Willow trees have even been added to the central pond to create a picturesque picnic area. As I pass by the beautifully swaying willows, their long, slender limbs dipping into the crystal blue water of the central pond, I make a mental note to make time for a picnic there later with Esse.

As much as she loves fish and willow trees, I am surprised she has not begged for me to have lunch there with her sooner.

Upon arriving at the manor's broad double doors, I notice the only family member present is Red, though he appears to be wrapped up in one of his car projects in the garage.

Since we put that lift in, he practically sleeps there. I remark amusedly to Kiro.

He has slept there. Smells like motor oil now. Kiro points out earning a laugh from me.

We should leave him be. I doubt Sela even mentioned why she was calling.

Kiro agrees and we make our way up the stairs to my office. Sensing the impending workload, an unenthusiastic Kiro pulls back into the depths of my mind, presumably to sleep. After ascending the wide oak steps to the second floor, I turn left and make my way to the end of the hall where the library is located. In the very back of the library, filled to the brim with first editions and old leather bounds, rests the arched doorway to my office.

Upon acquiring the property from a friend, one of my first decisions was to replace the glass door to the back room with a wooden door to make it a secured office. Red, being the handyman that he is, replaced the door for me, going so far as to craft the ornate object himself from an old oak tree that was damaged in a freak storm. With a final groan of protest, I unlock the heavy door, securing it behind me as I enter my darkened office.

Sela this better be important. Vegetarian or not, Esse makes the best food; I was desperately looking forward to today's lunch on the lawn.

I pick up the desk phone and unceremoniously plop into my chair to call my little sister. Leaning back in the black leather chair, I dial her number and wait. She picks up immediately, setting off alarms in the back of my head.

That was too fast. Wake up. I send a silent command to Kiro who reluctantly rouses himself inside my head.

"Kal?! What took you so long?" Sela's frantic voice bombards my sensitive ears from the other end of the phone.

"Calm down Sela, I was with Esse. She is excited about your upcoming visit by the way. Now, could you calmly tell me what is wrong?"

"You remember my last message to you, about that start-up pack causing problems for Carlos? We ran into a problem with them. Andre is injured. He is fine but Carlos is pissed and demands intervention. I am sure I do not need to tell you how bad it is that Andre was outmatched."

"How did this happen?" I question, the tension in my head growing exponentially as Sela's voice rises in pitch.

"We received our intel too late. Andre was informed by his contact that humans were going missing to the south of our

9

immediate territory and that a group of lycans had been seen in the area. Turns out, this prime-born by the name of Feng, a real triad asshole, is not killing humans, he is turning them. Andre was overwhelmed even with two of the brothers and three additional men."

"You are sure that this heir is turning the humans?" I demand in a worried tone, desperately wishing that Sela could be wrong but knowing inside that my baby sister is rarely wrong.

"It would be pretty hard for anyone to find that many impressionable lycanthropes just lying around big brother." Sela retorts in a fiery tone.

This is exactly what we need, a damn prime with a god complex turning humans into wolves. If left unchecked, he will surely bring the entire Order down on our heads.

No more picnic. Kiro chimes in, adding to my somber thoughts in his typically lupine, nonchalant manner.

Timing. I remind him.

"How many?" I ask Sela calmly.

"Andre said he counted more than twenty. Feng was not among them as far as he could tell, though we only have a vague description to go on. Definitely more newly made lycans than we can deal with directly."

"All right, you know the drill. Stay out of sight for a bit. Relocate if possible, especially until Andre is healed up. Tell the boss man I will make it up to him, we will make this right for him. I am going to call Don to get this situation straightened out. Stay safe, and be careful please, for my sake."

"Are you kidding? This is me we are talking about; I am always careful." My little sister retorts with childlike enthusiasm.

I can practically feel my impulsive baby sister grinning on the other end of the line. Her invincible aura fades quickly as she gives me the same warning.

"Take care brother and keep that fairy safe."

10

"Always," I assure her, ending the call before she can sense how truly worried I am.

I suppose I should call Don. This ordeal is shaping up to be a real pain in the ass. Esse will not be pleased.

With a deep sigh, I dial Don's current number. After six rings, he picks up.

"You are either calling me with great news or I am about to cancel my weekend plans." Don's deep, velvet voice answers unprompted.

"When do I ever call you with good news?" I inquire sarcastically.

"Fair point!" Don roars through rolling laughter. "So, what is it this time?"

"To put the situation bluntly, we have a prime causing problems. None of the usual players, a definite start-up."

"Shit. I am assuming if you are calling me, then he is either turning humans or is invading a declared territory without prior announcement. Any chance he is being subtle about it?" Don asks in his typically calm manner.

"Correct on both counts and no, it doesn't sound like he is being subtle at all. I do not know much about this guy other than the name, Feng, and that he supposedly has triad connections."

"That name matches with the Sun Yee. Their patriarch, Zhang, is a real piece of work. He holds the record for the greatest number of sons sired in the Chinese territories, which earns him respect amongst the families that comprise his sub-organizations. Zhang is the kind of lycan we are in the business of muzzling. Keeps a harem of well-domesticated females and his daughters sell for top price earning him a hefty fortune under the table. You know this story too well, no need for me to go on. I am certain this Feng character is one of his sons."

"Excellent, a welp with a daddy complex and too much money," I growl.

"Not necessarily, Zhang is your typical tyrant type; he values his sons and wants one of them to, one day, surpass him, but he does not intend to make it easy on them. He offers them no monetary aid and makes them settle all disputes through combat, sometimes to the death." Don explains casually.

"I see. So, this Feng will be one sick puppy. I don't suppose you could reach out, maybe arrange for a mutual location?" I inquire optimistically.

"I will see what I can do. I do not expect much effort to be required in bringing a man like Feng to the table. You have developed quite the reputation my friend; a chance to face off with you will surely be more than this Feng can resist."

I am left unsure of how to feel about Don's statement. On the one hand, stirring up the primes and their underlings was the plan from the start, but on the other hand, that was all planned out before I had something precious to lose. If Esse was to be injured or killed I would surely descend into the same madness that consumed my mother before her death. We lycans cannot live without our one partner for long.

As horrible as losing Esse would be for me, I also must consider what my death would do to her. Not only would she be emotionally destroyed, but there is also a decent chance her people would kill her for losing the keystone.

And now I officially have a headache.

"Thanks for the help Don, as usual, I owe you one." I sigh.

"Kal, while I have you here, there is another matter that could use your attention."

Great, because I was dying for more work.

Lazy. Kiro criticizes.

Ignoring my overly critical wolf, I urge Don to give me the bad news. "Lay it on me."

"Not to pile on, but Feng is not the only prime causing problems. The Italians and Germans are both growing restless and, as you know, they follow Serge who follows Gio, the current Italian prime. There is talk that the European sector, which is mostly controlled by Gio, is not too keen on human expansion of late. Cops are getting harder to pay off and we cannot seem to keep good wolves on the force these days. Keeping the humans in check and the wolves in line feels like putting out a fire with grease. I cannot say that I blame the Italians or their German underlings for their opinions on the matter; you know how I feel about the superiority complex of most humans. The European packs cannot let their wolves safely run anymore which is only going to add to the aggression and increased number of territorial disputes."

Don pauses pensively for a moment, which is highly unusual for the typically emboldened man.

"Then there is the Order. I do not need to tell you how problematic they have become." Don mutters in a low apologetic voice.

"I am painfully aware," I confirm. "We still have the Russians, Brazilians, and Africans on our side with Australia and Africa undecidedly neutral. That reminds me, Carlos is pissed. Feng caused quite a bit of damage for him." I inform Don.

"So, nothing has changed amongst our allies. I am assuming I must smooth things over with Carlos?" Don laughs, no doubt smirking on the other end of the phone like a clever fox.

"Please and thank you. As for the unrest, I am working on a solution for all of that. I have not forgotten our original arrangement from all those years ago." I assure the silver-haired man of mystery.

"It's a deal then. I will keep you informed my friend. Tell that fairy of yours I say hello, would you? I look forward to meeting her one of these days and hope she is adjusting well." Don's statement is one of genuine compassion. He has been nothing but considerate since Esse came to live with me.

"She is fine," I assure him quickly. "I will catch up with you later Don." With that, the call ends leaving me to my aching, thought-filled head.

Truthfully, I have barely had a moment to spare for acclimating Esse to the strange new world she was thrust into. Despite my lack of attention and the shock of losing her home of 980 years, Ellesse has proven to be a quick study. She has already mastered electricity, ridden in a cab, been on a plane, taken the bus, and adjusted to modern clothing. I have even taught her what and who the president is in our new home in Ireland. I am still trying to teach her how to use a cell phone, but for now, she communicates telepathically with Kiro who then relays the message to me.

She would rather use a carrier pigeon than a phone. Kiro points out, adding to the pounding pulse in my head.

Perhaps if you had not shown her what a carrier pigeon is, she would not be so resistant. I growl audibly despite my communication with Kiro being purely telepathic.

With a groan, I slump over the top of my antique mahogany desk, pressing the front of my face into my hands. The top of my desk is cluttered with paperwork, which is already piling up for the month. Consisting mostly of expense reports and various demands from the lycanthropes living within my territory, just the sight of the precariously stacked papers intensifies my headache.

I have never been good with paperwork or desk jobs. For me, such inconveniences are little more than a means to an end, another task to clutter up my already busy schedule.

No wonder my head constantly hurts, my to-do list is spiraling out of control.

Still resting my eyes in the palm of one hand, I free up the other to fish around in my pocket for my business cell phone. Turning the disposable phone on, I send one simple word simultaneously to five numbers, calling together my modest pack of misfits. Only Red's number responds, per protocol. I give him a time for tomorrow during which we will all meet here in the manor.

Having given Red the time for our meeting, I lay back in my chair, trusting in the silent lycan to disperse the message personally to the rest of our pack. Such complicated methods are essential for protecting my tiny family from the laundry list of enemies who would love nothing more than to see our heads on pikes. For the time being, only Red, Ellesse, Chiron, and I live on the manor grounds. Separating is safer for our family, therefore the others remain split up into small groups of two to three individuals.

Despite the small size of our pack, we are well established as one of the strongest of the territory holding packs globally. Among our motley crew we have: an engineer that specializes in coding, a sharpshooter with a mastery of every ranged weapon known to man, a surgeon who is also an omega, a mechanic who doubles as a carpenter and handyman, and a chemist who doubles as a world-class chef and terrifying warrior.

Our chef and chemist, Gus resides with our resident omega, Doc, who is also his partner. Together, the two of them can create an antidote to just about anything on the planet or create an untraceable toxin for all your poisoning needs.

Steak. Kiro adds, being a huge fan of Gus' T-bone steaks.

Dex, our resident engineer, lives with the best sharpshooter I have ever known, Annie, who is also his twin sister. We refer to them as the terrifying twins because the two of them together can bring down an entire military outpost without ever setting foot inside it.

Lastly, there is Red, our silent mechanic. He may not seem like much, but anything Red sets his mind to, will be accomplished to a standard of near perfection. Be it cars, construction, traps, or industrial machinery, Red can take it apart, put it together, and tell you how it works.

They may not be much to most, but to me, they are the best team anyone could ask for.

With a few hours to kill before Esse eats her dinner and the daunting piles of paperwork looming alongside the threat of a loose cannon prime, I decide to get down to work.

First things first, a quick call to Ivan to clean up the situation in Europe. He should be more than happy to throw his weight around in Europe again.

As the Russian prime, Ivan Kuznetsov has an undeniable reason to maintain an interest in the European territory. Because of Russia's size in comparison to the other territories, which typically encompass multiple countries, the span of Ivan's land has been limited. An agreement was made during the last gathering of the primes, before our unity broke down, that Russia would occupy only the country from which its territorial name is derived.

Perhaps that is why he agreed to align himself with me so quickly. The unity of the primes works in his favor as it allows Ivan to compensate for his reduced territory with wealth by means of exclusive trade rights with other prime families. Perhaps I can strike a deal with Ivan to provide security at our meeting with Feng.

Do we trust? Kiro inquires.

For now, we have no choice. Depending upon the number of humans he has turned, this Feng character may be more than we can deal with. I inform my inquisitive wolf.

With the matter decided, I dial Ivan from the desk phone. Despite my headache, I breeze through the phone call, most of the minor paperwork, and balancing the week's expenditures in a few hours. The phone call with Ivan, though brief, is productive and he agrees to send a team of six to the manor in anticipation of the upcoming meeting. He also assures me that the situation in Europe will be dealt with, which puts my restless mind at ease.

With the arrangements handled and some paperwork out of the way, I push myself sluggishly from my well-worn desk chair and make my way down to the dining room for dinner. Before I reach the bottom of the stairs, I can tell that Gus is in the kitchen working his magic.

Strange that I did not hear him come in.

Stranger that you did not smell him. Steak? Kiro growls hungrily from the back of my mind, our shared headache finally dissipating.

Steak it is, but with veggies. We have pressed our luck enough with Esse today.

Kiro grumbles his reluctant agreement as we head for the kitchen. The dark mahogany door to the manor's stainless-steel kitchen sits propped open, presumably to prevent the hell-pit of a room from reaching inferno-grade temperatures. As I push past the door and into the kitchen, I lightly knock on the door frame to announce myself.

"Hey Gus, you seen Esse yet?" I inquire, attempting to silence my growling stomach.

The burly Irishman rounds the corner at the end of the steel countertop, a stained rag in his hand and characteristically broad smile upon his face.

"Not yet, eh. Pretty sure Red's given' the lass a lesson on the internal combustion engine." Gus laughs, wiping his hands on the rag.

"That sounds about right." I laugh along with the intimidating, russet-red bearded Irishman.

That is my Esse, always trying to understand the inner workings of the world around her, no matter how complex or simple.

The image of Esse attempting to understand the composition of the internal combustion engine reminds me of her first flight on an airplane. For someone who flies every day at speeds that would appear as a blur to the human eye, she had no faith in the ability of an engineered aircraft to carry her over a single ocean to my home in Ireland from the Eastern coast of Canada. The entire flight was spent with a trembling Esse burrowed deeply into her seat like a frightened child.

Come to think of it, I did have to settle for eighteen as the age on her false ID and passport. The shifter we got the paperwork from insisted that fifteen would pass better through ID checks, but I refuse to treat her like a child in public. It is bad enough that I can scarcely touch her outside the manor without drawing the attention of strangers.

Pervert. Kiro growls, thinking himself clever.

17

Laugh now but if we are placed on some government list you will not be laughing then. I remind him.

"Gus, would you mind making me a plate?" I ask him hopefully.

"Consider it done, sir." He answers in his thick Ulster accent.

Gus turns to retrieve a plate from one of the standing cabinets on the far side of the kitchen. I watch hungrily as he carefully heaps the ivory plate full of mashed potatoes, steak, beans, and his famous homemade bread. He then walks the plate back down the kitchen line to me.

"Thanks, Gus, I appreciate your efforts."

"Can't have you eaten' slop ever' night now," Gus informs me, brandishing the serving spoon like a cross parent scolding his child.

I flash Gus a grateful smile and retreat from the kitchen with my plate in hand. The next door on the left leads to the ornate dining room stocked with an entire wall of china cabinets and oriental hutches filled to the brim with fine porcelain and china plates. More than six sets of decorative silverware stock the drawers of the cabinets, which match the three large dining tables to perfection.

I take my place at the end of the closest table and begin silently eating my meal, hoping to at least finish the meat before Ellesse arrives for dinner.

Maybe if she does not see meat on my plate tonight, she will go easy on me when I catch her up on everything that is happening. I think hopefully, though I know inside that Esse will not be happy to hear about such complications.

She will not stay. Kiro points out in clear agitation.

We will do our best to make her stay here but we cannot force her to stay. If she insists upon being at the meeting, we will simply take measures to keep her safe. I remind Kiro.

Though Kiro is not as aggressive as most lycan's wolves, he has struggled over the years to balance my somewhat passive nature and keep us both safe in a world that does not permit pacifists. The result has been a steady increase in Kiro's aggressive tendencies, something that is only mitigated by Esse's presence or long runs and swims.

I know you want to keep her safe, but not by forcing her to be a prisoner all over again. You know that would kill her. I reason telepathically with the temperamental lupine.

Fine. Suggestions? He asks wryly.

Before I have a chance to lay out a strategy for convincing Esse to remain in the safety of the manor, the excitable fairy rushes into the dining room carrying her bowl of rabbit food.

"Am I late?" She exclaims cheerfully, hurriedly taking a seat beside me.

"Not at all," I assure her, trying not to sound nervous.

She wastes no time seeking answers. "So, what did Sela have to say today?"

Esse does not bother to lift her gaze from her bowl of assorted greens and vegetables as she waits for answers I do not wish to give her.

"Can we not eat first?" I plead, attempting to redirect her focus to food.

She stops eating. "Kal, like it or not, whatever happens to you affects me too. Furthermore, you owe me for missing lunch, a lunch that I worked very hard on."

"I swear I was excited about lunch; you know that. Vegetarian or not, your food is amazing. Even more so when you consider that you spent your entire life hidden away from modern civilization and any form of kitchen appliance."

"Says the wolf who scarfed down a steak to avoid answering me." Esse retorts.

"If I were a lesser wolf then you would be on your back for that remark," I grumble, annoyed at her cleverness.

"The fact that you are who you are is why I love you." She states plainly.

"So, you trust me to keep you informed but safe?" I probe cautiously.

"Of course, I trust you; and if you trust me, then you will keep me…how do you put it…in the loop." She gives a casual wave of her hand, knowing that she has me backed into a corner.

Despite my compromising position, I smile in appreciation of Esse's ferocity. Her bold nature is exactly why I love her.

"As always, you are right." I sigh in defeat. "We have encountered a problem, one that could prove dangerous. I explained to you once that there are nine original prime families, with Australia and America being the newest established families and territories. A descendant from one of these families by the name of Feng is turning humans. Presumably, he is raising an army, though we do not know the reason behind his actions at this time." I explain cautiously.

"No."

"No?" I raise an eyebrow at Esse's overly simplified response.

"You intend to deal with this problem head-on and I am saying no. Your methods are too reckless, and you do not have the numbers to face an army. Besides, such reckless behavior from both parties will draw attention." Esse reasons skillfully, her mind made up on the subject.

How did I not see this reaction coming?

"Esse I do not have a choice this time. If Feng continues to grow his army, I will be the first one he comes for. Our only chance is to stop this now. Do not worry, I will have a careful plan in place. I have already called Don and Ivan as well. I assure you; we have the resources we need."

"Then this mess should be handled in time for the holiday. What do we do?" Esse asks calmly.

Here we go. Buckle up mighty wolf because I will be throwing you under the bus if I must.

I will tell her otherwise. Kiro counters, seemingly unphased by my threat.

"My little fairy, this situation calls for neutral ground and I was hoping you would go easy on me and stay here in the manor where you are safest. Perhaps Chiron could come over and watch a movie with you." I suggest, attempting to soften the blow of my suggestion.

"You know me better than that, Kal." Esse sets down her fork, having finished eating, and turns to face me fully.

Dead. Kiro whimpers. *We are so dead.*

"If any of the primes not currently allied with us were to be made aware that you exist, you would become the sole target for their violence. I will not risk that." I try desperately to remain calm despite the growing fear that I might lose everything.

For a single, drawn-out, moment Esse remains still and silent, like a gargoyle guarding a cathedral. When she finally speaks, the serene tone of her voice takes me by surprise.

"You know that I am uniquely qualified to understand your situation and your concerns for my safety; but you are the one who taught me that all relationships, even those between fae, are based on compromise. Just because we non-humans feel love for one creature eternally does not mean we just stop putting in effort for the sake of that creature. Are you not the one who is always pushing the females are equals regime? I know that you want to keep me safe but sticking me here under guard is not the way. Is it even any safer for me to be here than it is for me to be with you? By now the rumor has spread that you found someone; granted they likely assume me to be a lycanthrope. Why can we not use their assumptions to our advantage?"

I am taken aback by Esse's flawless reasoning but feel compelled to assess her logic more thoroughly.

"What do you mean?" I pry. "How might we use this assumption to our advantage?"

"Well, I am only asking to be present, just in case something was to go sideways. That does not mean I must show my face." Esse points out with a triumphant grin.

Risky. Kiro points out.

I agree, there is a high level of risk involved in this plan if we can even call it a plan. However, she has a point; if we leave her here, she would still be vulnerable. Additionally, leaving Esse here would mean leaving Doc here to watch out for her and that would leave us with no healer and no early warning system. Besides, knowing Esse, she would find her way out of the manor and get herself in trouble trying to navigate the public transit system on her own.

With a weighted sigh, I push my plate away. "You win. After all, you make some decent points. I will not attempt to prohibit you from coming with us. However, in return for my respecting your need to be involved, you will respect my need to keep you safe. Therefore, there will be rules, the same rules that all the others of the pack follow. From the point of our arrival at the location Don provides, you will listen to every word I say without complaint. In fact, it will be safer for all parties if you do not speak at all while we are there, especially once Feng has arrived. You will also be hiding your ears. Agreed?"

"Agreed." She nods, seemingly content with our arrangement.

That was not as bad as I thought.

"Sela is still coming for the Fall Moon Feast, right?" Esse asks worriedly.

"Of course. She would not miss it for anything."

Pumpkins. Kiro reminds me.

I will not forget your precious pumpkins. I assure him.

"You are talking to Kiro right now," Esse observes.

"He wanted to make sure we remembered the pumpkins," I inform my inquisitive fairy.

"How could a fairy forget something as important as the pumpkins?" she asks in mock outrage. "I knew that I would never hear the end of it if I did not come through with the pumpkins."

22

"I do not know how Kiro got stuck on this idea of bobbing for pumpkins in the lake near the hunting grounds. I informed him that apples would be easier, but he insists on pumpkins." I shake my head in amusement.

"I am afraid it is my fault entirely. I asked Red what Halloween is. Some people from another place were talking about it at the store the other day. I guess I got excited and shared what I had learned with Kiro while you were asleep." Esse shrugs sheepishly.

"Of course, the two of you would think up something like this." I laugh audibly at their childlike wonder.

You would never know these two creatures held so much power between them by the way they act.

Esse finally pushes back from the table and I reach out to take her bowl and my plate. With the day almost over, I may finally have a calm moment to spend with just Esse.

Gus calls out for me from the back of the kitchen as I bring the plates to the dish area. "About tomorrow, Doc's going to be a bit late. She could not get out of her shift at the hospital."

"Not a problem Gus. She can sit this one out. Just be sure to fill her in later for me."

"Of course." Gus agrees. "I have to ask lad, is my lass still safe?"

I turn and place a hand securely on Gus' shoulder, craning my neck back to look directly into his face. "I made you both a promise the day you joined this family and I intend to keep it. Even if keeping my word to you should cost me my life or my chance at achieving my objective, your lives matter more to me than anything else. I owe you both that much."

Gus nods slowly, his eyes apologetic. I need no words from him to know what he is feeling. Gus, like most of us, is torn between wanting to change things for the better and wanting to protect what he has now.

Perhaps if someone had shared this sentiment back then our parents would still be alive.

Then we would not be us. Kiro points out, acknowledging the impact that my parents' deaths have had on my journey so far.

Pushing aside my thoughts of doom and gloom, I round the corner back into the hall off of which the dining room and kitchen are found. The last thing I need is for Esse to worry about my mental state right now. For everything that is to come, I will be relying on Esse's calm demeanor and level head.

She and the winged one can work on decorations tomorrow. Kiro offers.

That is brilliant. A hassle-free means of keeping Esse occupied while we sort out logistics. I praise the clever wolf.

"So, what will it be tonight?" I ask Esse lightheartedly, leaning against the wooden doorframe to the kitchen.

"Red told me about this one about a wizard child with a white owl who rides a broom and saves the world from an evil wizard. He says there are all kinds of mythical creatures in it, maybe even faeries! Do we have that one?" Esse chirps excitedly, unknowingly describing the *Harry Potter* movies.

"Yes, we have them. That is actually a series of several books that were made into movies." I grin, biting back a laugh at how little Esse knows of popular culture and modern era literature and movies.

"Excellent!" Esse exclaims, clapping her hands together happily. She flies, literally, over the table and lands lightly in front of me.

"You go get it and I will turn the TV box on." Esse bounces between the balls and heels of her feet excitedly, hardly able to contain herself at the prospect of a movie that may or may not contain faeries.

Before I can respond, she turns and dashes toward the stairs, scarcely bothering to run up the stairs as she propels herself forward with self-generated wind.

"Esse, perhaps you should wait and let me work the television?" I call after her worriedly, imagining the ease with which she could accidentally destroy my television or our bedroom.

"I have seen you do it dozens of times." She calls back over her shoulder to me with a smile on her face. "I think I can handle it."

I suppose if she is determined...how much damage could she do? I ask Kiro telepathically.

Kiro's lack of response concerns me. With a myriad of horrific images in my head, I make my way quickly to the media room. The manor's rather spacious media room is a clear favorite among the family. Inside the room, we have every game imaginable, a pool table, an air hockey table, a dart lane, a small bowling alley with two lanes, a ping-pong table, a table for blackjack and poker games, and three vintage pinball machines. In the very back of the room, near the bowling lanes, rests a modest door leading to the not-so-modest home theatre.

I make my way through the array of games toward the theatre, thankful that we took the time to alphabetize our hundreds of DVDs. Having been in the small room every night since bringing Esse home, I know exactly where to go to find what I am looking for, despite the wall-to-wall shelves filled with stacks upon stacks of DVDs. I decide to take the entire set with me as Esse will likely be up watching them all night. With the disks securely in hand, I hurry back out of the room, closing the doors and turning off the lights behind me as I go.

The media room rests directly behind the left staircase leading to the second floor, making my ascent to our bedroom quick and easy. I find myself practically running the last few lengths of the upstairs hallway to the third-floor staircase.

Please let the third floor and the roof be there; that is all I ask.

No explosions yet. Kiro informs me lazily as we arrive on the third floor.

Our bedroom rests at the end of the third-floor corridor with the various other bedrooms on the floor consisting entirely of guest bedrooms. The door to the room is ajar upon our arrival, left open by Esse in her excitement to reach the television.

I peak my head cautiously inside, feeling like a duck about to be blown away by a man with a rifle. Inside, Esse is half-tucked behind the television grumbling angrily to herself.

"Looks like you could use a hand little fairy." I smile, hoping that she will not blast me through the door for insinuating she cannot finish this task herself.

"No way. I can get this to work, I know I can." She insists sharply, a bundle of cables clutched in her right hand.

Best to let her tire herself out. Kiro suggests helpfully.

Agreed.

I set the DVDs down on the corner of the bed and stretch out atop the quilted comforter, my hands tucked behind my head as I watch Esse continue her technological massacre. I cannot help but admire her determination.

Among the hundreds of other traits that I love about Ellesse, her fierce determination must be among the top five, alongside her uninhibited curiosity, unyielding sense of individuality, unending compassion, and utter lack of fear. After losing her home and Bartro, Esse and Chiron, her second, came to live with me in a land neither of them had ever seen or imagined. Just getting Chiron, with his brilliant green-blue wings, here to Ireland from across an ocean proved problematic.

Chiron has to fly alone across the sea using special runic charms and careful use of his wings to remain hidden from both the boats below him and planes above him. Such lengthy camouflaged flights take an unimaginable toll on the ani of the fairy, leaving them in a weakened state for days afterward.

In hindsight, that might be why Harlequin, the fairy king, seemed so weak after flying to Canada from South America.

26

After the arduous journey, Chiron had to be driven carefully through pre-selected toll routes to ensure his wings would not be seen. Luckily, we primes keep stringently maintained pipelines of well-compensated human employees in various positions to keep our travels under the radar. We maintain a payroll of various police officers, toll booth attendants, forestry servicemen and women, military officials, and hospital staff to keep our activities discrete in the modern era.

Poor Chiron has to remain under wraps in a hunting cabin toward the heart of the property by the lake. His adjustment to human society after centuries of isolation has been more strenuous than Esse's. After all, Esse had Kiro and me to help ease her into things while Chiron had to ease himself into the world from the sidelines. Not having wings yet also made the adjustment much easier for Esse.

Despite her less-than-ideal introduction to humanity at the hands of the Order, Esse has not lost her interest in all things human. She loves nothing more than to go shopping or sightseeing, taking in every sight and sound that she can find of the world around her. The simplest objects that those of us born into this world take for granted are like treasures to Esse, who has taken to hoarding such objects in our room. Looking around I can identify several empty bottles and cans, a stack of tourist pamphlets and maps, at least a dozen coffee mugs and keychains, and her growing assortment of bottle caps, pins, and stickers. Seeing her menagerie of items brings a smile to my face.

To have such a view of the world is something I would give my very soul for.

May she never see the things we have. Kiro agrees.

With a huff, Esse finally gives up. She sits back on her folded knees with her arms crossed in frustration over her chest. Esse's shoulder-length silver curls, which can be spotted in even the most crowded of venues, fall haphazardly into her face, completing her patented look of mock anger.

I sit up and ready myself to spend the next five to ten minutes putting our television back in working order.

"How about you take five and get changed for bed. I will have it up and running by the time you get back." I assure an exceptionally pouty Esse.

"This is not over." She hisses at the television as she gets up and makes her way to our walk-in closet, which has become her personal dressing room.

I set to work plugging the cords back into their appropriate locations, turning on the television, and starting up the DVD player. Just as I manage to pull everything together, Esse reappears from her closet wearing an old classic of hers: a tattered white linen-cotton blend dress worn so thin with age that it moves like silk. The poor garment has grown so worn with time that Esse now uses it only to sleep in, fearful that it will fall apart at any moment.

Like a faithful friend, Esse's classic white dress has followed her throughout her life. That dress is the only remaining garment of her original set of clothes carried from the Amazon to the Northern Woods in Canada over 900 years ago. The tiny white dress is older than Canada itself, having been carefully mended over time as holes have worn into the natural fabric. Like Esse, the dress has withstood so much and seen so little.

"Ready for movie time?" I ask Esse over my shoulder, still crouched in front of the media setup.

"Absolutely!" Esse chirps excitedly, worming her way under the comforter and linen sheet.

"Comfy?" I laugh as she finally settles herself, like a puppy arranging its favorite blanket.

She nods as I place the DVD in the tray and press start. Finally, it is my turn to get ready for bed after a long day. My process, thankfully, is much simpler than Esse's. I tug off my t-shirt and ditch the worn-out work jeans, which could probably use a wash, before plopping down beside Esse.

She is already fully invested in the film, which has just started to play, leaving me playing the role of spectator and, occasionally, the narrator as I explain the minor details of the film that are still foreign to her. Though doing so obstructs her view, I pull Esse closer to me. Having her close enough to feel her pulse and breathing soothes Kiro and me, making sleep easier during the night hours when lycanthropes typically like to be awake and hunting.

Come to think of it, being physically close to Esse has always had a pacifying effect on us. I realize. *We need all the calm we can get these days.* I acknowledge internally.

Decorations. Kiro reminds me of our earlier scheme to keep Esse occupied.

"Do you think you could do me a huge favor tomorrow?" I ask cautiously.

"What kind of favor?" Esse throws me a suspicious sideways glance before returning her focus to the movie.

"I have some business stuff to attend to tomorrow, but Kiro is concerned about the festival décor. Do you think you and Chiron could work a bit of fairy magic on the hunting grounds where the feast is going to be served and the games are going to take place? The lake could use a fairy touch honestly."

Esse looks up from her movie at me quizzically, searching my face for signs of treachery.

"I think we could manage that." She finally answers, satisfied with my apparent lack of ulterior motive.

I suppress a sigh of relief, knowing that Esse would blow a hole through the side of our room if she suspected for a second that I was sidelining her.

"Wonderful! That's my helpful little fairy." I smile, genuinely happy to have her help on this matter. I grab Esse abruptly, not giving her the chance to protest, and roll her playfully onto my chest.

"Kal!" she complains. "The movie?"

"DVDs are not one-use items Esse. We can watch it later." I laugh.

Though she rolls her eyes I know I have won once again, resulting in a very pleasant end to a stressful day.

Two

After a brief and baconless breakfast with Ellesse, I head back upstairs to the third floor to ready myself for today's meeting which will occur in the manor's most insulated and naturally noisy room, the media room. Despite the urgency of today's meeting, I am dragging my feet. Knowing that this would be the case, I gave myself extra time to get ready this morning, taking great care to wake up early and have my jacket and clothes set aside for the day before going to sleep the night before.

Meetings like this are almost as bad as paperwork. I groan internally. *If I had it my way, someone else would be running things around here, but the goals I have in mind require me to possess a certain degree of authority. I could never ask Red, or anyone else, to assume the risk of the role I have taken on.* I remind myself, recognizing the importance of the tasks before me.

Having grabbed my jacket, keys, and phone, I make my way back down to my office on the second floor. Closing the door to both the library and the office behind me, I take special care to be discrete about my business today. A quick scan by Kiro tells me it is safe to open the locked drawer in the bottom of the ornate desk using a vintage skeleton key that stays hidden in a secret panel of the bookshelf in my bedroom at all times.

Inside the drawer rests several files containing information on each of the current prime families as well as their ancestors and known descendants. I leaf through the yellowish documents and locate the file on the Sun Yee family. Though I already know that the file contains no information on Feng, the documents within the file do mention Zhang, whom we now assume is Feng's father, as well as the rest of the triad. Unfortunately, not many of Zhang's heirs are listed by name as he has sired too many to track.

I pull the file and hurriedly replace the others so that I can close and lock the drawer. Keeping the files in view for too long puts me on edge; most probably because one of these files contains the story of my own family.

Trying not to dwell on such thoughts, I backtrack to my room once more with the file tucked securely under my jacket. I replace the key in the false panel behind three large leatherbound books sitting upon the top shelf of my oak bookshelf. The panel is perfectly hidden behind the large volumes with only Esse and me knowing of its location.

With nothing else to delay my leaving the comfort of my bedroom, I turn and abandon the safety of the master suite. As the door closes quietly behind my back, something inside me screams to turn around and simply ignore the impending faceoff with Feng, in the hopes that he will simply ignore me and my rag-tag family.

He will not. Kiro informs me with a certainty that makes my skin crawl.

Projected in Kiro's mind is an image of how he would play out the situation from Feng's perspective. The images of Kiro singling out the most vulnerable individuals among the family both unnerves and enrages me.

I will not give this second-rate prime the chance to isolate members of our family. Perhaps we should bring them into the manor until we receive the green light from Don? I suggest telepathically.

No. This one is reckless. He will not plan as I do. Stay the course. Kiro suggests.

Then how do you know he will not simply stay clear of us? I pry, delving into Kiro's predatory logic.

Because he is a coward. Feng will build his army until he outnumbers us twenty to one. Kiro reasons.

Having never failed me to this point, I follow Kiro's instructions and make a mental note to remind everyone to utilize caution without breaking routine in the coming days. I reach the door to the media room and hesitate for one final moment before reaching a steady hand out to open the door. Without needing to open the door first, I can easily discern the individuals behind it as well as their specific locations.

Red is leaning casually against the pool table while Annie and Dex sit at the poker table. More specifically, Annie, our resident sharpshooter, sits on the poker table in keeping with her typically rebellious nature. Gus stands alone, casually throwing darts with pinpoint accuracy at the farthest dartboard. Looking around at the odd assemblage of lycans in the media room, one would never know that each creature gathered here is as lethal as a small army.

Gus, despite being a gentle giant, spent the first five hundred years of his lifespan as an enforcer for one of the deadliest primes in lycanthrope history. The bearded charmer carries a bloody reputation for having ended the lives of more than a thousand lycans and humans.

The twins, Annie and Dex, watched their parents die for failing to turn Annie over to their alpha and lived the next fifty years on the run from the notorious German alpha, Serge. In those fifty years, Annie has mastered the use of every ranged weapon known to man. She can make a bomb out of most household items and a gun out of spare parts.

Dex is equally formidable, though his strength lies primarily in guerrilla combat methods and strategy. Dex is notorious for taking out defenses and crippling large numbers of enemies from a distance, allowing Annie to swoop in and finish the job. Even so, Dex is not one to shy away from getting his hands dirty when necessary, especially when it comes to protecting his sister. Despite their skills, both twins retain an innocence that the rest of us lack, primarily because of their young age.

Then there is Red. No one knows his story aside from me, and even I do not know much of him. What I do know is that Red was a high-ranking member of a satellite pack under the umbrella of the Italian primes before his entire pack was mysteriously massacred one night after the death of a young male. Red does not talk much about the incident, but Don has hinted at times that the young male was Red's partner and that his death sent Red into a blind rage during which he single-handedly slaughtered his entire pack.

"Cutting it close again." Red remarks casually as I enter the familiar room, the carefree auras of my family laced with only the slightest edge of tension.

Gus pauses his dart-throwing to flash me a warm grin. Dex leans casually back in his chair and gives a nonchalant wave of his hand while Annie remains completely unphased, her legs swinging casually over the side of the dark, velvet topped table.

"How are things at the station Annie?" I ask casually.

Annie shrugs. "Business as usual. Everything seems quiet on the streets these days; it's honestly rather boring."

I stifle a laugh at Annie's constant need for adventure and adrenaline. "I suppose I can sleep easier with you on the force these days, officer Annie."

She bristles predictably at my teasing insult but does not bother to retaliate.

The part of me that views Annie as a little sister cannot help but tease her. Annie spent the first twelve years of her life hidden away in a series of tunnels; from the time she was old enough to crawl until her alpha discovered her existence. The poor female would likely have gone feral had her brother not started bringing her books and toys to brighten her spirits, despite his parents' warning that seeing her would only lead their pack to Annie. In the end, their parents were right to warn Dex as he was followed one day on his way to see his twin sister. Three days later their alpha demanded his parents turn them over; when the twins' parents, instead, told them to run, their alpha beheaded both parents and ripped out their hearts for good measure. This tragic tale is how Annie earned the nickname: the girl in the cave.

"So, what's going down that calls for you to gather us all up like this? You know how George gets when I take days off from the tech shop." Dex inquires cleverly, having been given no details on the situation yet.

"This should not take long," I assure him as I take a seat in one of the loungers in the right corner of the room near the door.

"I got a call from Sela. Apparently, a man by the name of Feng, who we think is the son of the Chinese prime Zhang, is stirring up trouble in the Americas."

"Was Carlos unwilling to take care of it?" Dex asks in confusion, knowing that the Americas are far outside our territorial boundary.

"He tried. Carlos sent Andre and a fair number of others to put this Feng fella back in line not realizing who he was. Feng got the better of them. From what I gather, they were lucky to return home at all; Andre was met with an army."

"An army!" Annie tenses. "We do not have the weaponry to take on an army Kal." Annie shakes her head in dismay.

"Relax lass, I'm sure the lad knows that already." Gus chimes in on my behalf.

"I have already made some calls to Ivan and Don. Ivan is sending a team of six. They will be well-armed. Don has even managed to find us a neutral location, he just has to get Feng to agree to meet there. This is why we formed the coalition in the first place, to deal with threats like this as a collective. None of this is to say we are in for a cakewalk, but the odds are far better for us than they were for Andre. Ideally, we will be settling this peacefully."

"Peaceful resolution seems unlikely," Red interjects.

"Hence the need for countermeasures," I assure him through gritted teeth. "Let me reiterate for everyone that no one is forced to face situations like this with me. I promised each of you a better, safer life here in this family and I intend to keep that promise. If any one of you wishes to sit this one out or run while your anonymity is still assured, no one will stop you." I assure everyone.

No one budges.

"We know you are true to your word. I think I speak for ever'one when I say that we are with ya all the way." Gus adds, reminding me of just how far he has come in life.

Gus was originally tasked with the enforcement of territorial laws upon the satellite packs that comprised his prime's territory. One day, several decades ago, he was given a new task guarding a captive he had never seen. This mysterious captive was kept isolated in solitary confinement, sheltered even from Gus until one day this captive made an escape attempt. That is how Gus met Doc; as fate would have it, she was his captive.

Gus' alpha had been keeping Doc locked away to use her gifts of sight and healing for his gain. As an omega, Doc retains rare bloodline-based abilities passed down from her mother's side. In her rare case, Doc was gifted with multiple abilities making her highly prized and a valuable asset to any prime.

From the moment Gus laid eyes on Doc he knew his killing days were numbered. He was backed into a corner that day; he could not bring himself to kill Doc but knew that if he did not return her to captivity that they both would be mercilessly hunted. Like my father, the burly Irishman chose to run, only he thought his plan through a bit farther. Gus faked an accident to temporarily throw his alpha off their scent. The bold tactic worked just long enough for Gus and Doc to make their way here to me in Ireland, where Gus was born many centuries before. My reputation proceeded me even then.

"None of us thought this would be easy," Dex murmurs breaking through my distracted musing. "We are all here because we share your desire for a better life and a safer world for the ones we love." Dex throws a thoughtful glance toward his sister.

"Agreed," Red adds.

"That is all fine and good, but if we are going to do this, we have work to do." Annie points out sternly, never one to wear her emotions on her sleeve.

"Agreed. Annie, you and Dex are two of the most brilliant strategists I have ever known. Surely, between the two of you, we will be able to plan for any contingency."

My words seem to perk Annie up a bit. She has never been one to turn down a challenge or a compliment of her skills as a strategist.

"We will see what we can do." She grins, throwing a sly glance toward Dex over her shoulder. "So, tell me what we have on this guy."

I pass her the file on the Chinese primes. Most of the information contained within the file references Zhang and his oldest son, though there is a list of other known relatives with almost no information on the individuals themselves.

"This is it?" Annie growls in clear disdain. She looks up at me with a mix of confusion and frustration. "Feng is not even mentioned. Can we even be sure he is one of Zhang's descendants?" Annie asks as she sifts once more through the thin file.

"We must work on that assumption for the time being. His origin should not affect our contingency protocols. Regardless of his ancestry, we need to assume that Feng can par-shift and we have verified that he can pass the genetic structure on to humans, effectively creating an army."

"An army he may or may not have control of," Annie murmurs thoughtfully.

"I have Don looking into the background on this guy as much as possible. If there is anything more for us to know about him, we will know it soon." I add.

Annie shoots me an exasperated glare through narrowed eyes. "You know I cannot count the number of contingencies forming for the situation with just what we know so far. If I pull this off, you may as well hail me as a god." She informs me cynically.

"Do I not do that already?" I attempt to defuse the time-bomb that is Annie with a clever grin.

"You could stand to do it a bit more often." Annie shrugs.

"Just to cover our bases here, this means you can get us ready in time?" I ask the now musing sharpshooter.

"Do not insult us, boss. You know full well that the two of us can do damn near anything. We will have a contingency plan within a contingency plan for you as well as a list of required *materials* for this little scheme of ours. We will be needing the layout of the venue in advance, of course. Three days should be enough notice for us to work our magic. If at all possible, I will be wanting to put eyes on every angel of the place beforehand. I should be able to borrow the tech I need for that project from work. Just remember, if we break it, we buy it, and by *we*, I do mean *you*, boss man." Dex informs me in the form of a laundry list of demands.

"Excellent. Let us try not to have to buy the expensive tech this time then. Assume, for now, that the location will resemble the warehouse."

Annie nods her approval and hops lightly off of her perch on the poker table.

I glance at the clock on the wall near the door and notice that the hour is growing late. "Annie, be careful not to miss your shift." I remind her.

She nods and heads for the door, waving goodbye to her brother as she goes.

"As for the rest of you, I have another task of great importance. Esse will be present during this meeting." I inform everyone.

"That is a royally stupid idea." Dex asserts.

"I am aware, but you try telling a fairy armed with the power of a natural disaster that she cannot do something." I counter calmly.

"All I am asking is for your assistance in keeping Esse safe. Red, I am thinking I will put her somewhere where she cannot be seen or sensed. If you do not object, I will use your scent to hide her location; mine would draw too much attention. Dex, all I need from you is one of your earpieces delegated to use for Esse to listen in so that she does not drop her guard to hone in on our auras. I need her ready to flee if needed."

"I suppose one more earpiece will not matter." Dex agrees.

"No objections here." Red nods.

"Then there is one final matter, and I will make it quick. I am sure everyone is aware by now that Carlos is bringing his brothers, my sister, Andre, and several other non-relatives to visit for this year's feast. I cannot stress enough the importance of this year's festivities. I know some here may still have trust issues concerning the other primes of our coalition, but we cannot see our goals achieved alone. Sela and Andre, two of our own, trust Carlos and that is good enough for me. Don is taking care of security for us so that we may all enjoy the festivities without worry; he is calling in every favor he has with the local government including law enforcement, military, the works. No one should be bothering us even if one of the neighborhoods nearby should notice something irregular." I explain carefully, hoping my comrades grasp the severity of the situation without dreading the coming holiday.

"What about Ivan?" Red asks, seemingly chatty today for such a notoriously silent man.

"He has business to attend to, but the invitation has been extended and he may very well make an appearance."

"Don't worry, we can play nice," Dex assures me lightheartedly.

"I know you can. None of you have ever let me down before. Gus, how are we doing with the menu? Do you have everything you need?" I turn my attention to the chef of the hour who has been busily preparing the menu for the feast for the last three weeks.

"Keeping it traditional o'course. Should have the truck here the week before it's needed with ever'thing on it I need." Gus' distinguishingly thick Irish accent intensifies with excitement as he speaks of the cooking preparations.

"And the beer?" Dex perks up, focusing on the one thing that matters most to him about this festival.

"Aye, took care of the drink I did. Do you even need to ask lad?" Gus shakes his head mockingly at Dex as the lean, blonde-haired analyst devolves into fits of laughter.

"Well, it sounds like everything is well in hand." I declare. "Everyone rest up for what is to come, both the good and the bad. Be ready to head out within the next couple of days. I will try to give as much notice as possible."

With the meeting concluded and no further business to attend to, everyone disperses, fleeing the media room like rats fleeing a sinking ship.

Finally. Decorations now? Lunch too. Kiro demands in disjointed thoughts, his mind focused squarely on thoughts of Esse, food, and pumpkins.

You are always thinking with your stomach. I point out.

Better than you always thinking with your. . .

Watch it Kiro! I end that train of thought before it can begin. *So help me, a bit of mental privacy would be nice.*

Kiro sulks bitterly, stewing over the fact that such aspects of life are exclusively mine given the lack of canine anatomy among faeries.

Forget I said anything. Why don't we just go enjoy some lunch? Maybe we will get lucky and both of us will get what we want.

Kiro laughs, never one to stay angry or downtrodden for too long.

Three

I waste no time in retrieving the Gator from the shed. The small vehicle would normally be unnecessary given the power of the four-legged Kiro. However, with the Order's increased activity and hunting on private property on the rise, running in wolf form is no longer safe. Less than fifty years ago it was commonplace for lycans lucky enough to possess large properties to run in wolf form on their lands. Most lycans would either carry tiny packs containing spare clothes around their neck and chest or stash the tiny bundles around the property. That was before the age of technology; before drones and camera phones were everywhere. Now our wolves rarely see the light of the moon with their own eyes.

So, I am forced to resort to traveling by tiny, motorized vehicle or on foot across the manor grounds. Being the pampered creature I am, I decide to take the Gator rather than trek the quarter-mile on foot to the lake, with Kiro pouting the entire way.

With the all-terrain vehicle fired up, Kiro and I steer toward the old hiking path, which is a hunting trail utilized by the wolves upon rare occasions to relieve stress. The woods of the property, like most of Ireland, are relatively sparse grasslands with occasional patches of thick brush and tall trees. Most of the land around the manor was nothing more than open fields with rocky spines crisscrossing the landscape until Don took possession of the land nearly fifty years ago.

Don was smart enough to plan for the age of technology and create a safe space for my pack to live and carry out our plans for the future. Though no tree on the property stands more than twelve feet tall, and few have a trunk size thicker than my waist, the land is slowly healing. Chiron, upon arrival in his new home, was also kind enough to grow up some of the trees around the lake for us, making our hunting grounds a bit more secure.

If not for fae like Don and Chiron, there would not be enough land to go around, especially wooded land.

I push such thoughts from my mind, telling myself that we will find an answer to the troubles plaguing our world one day.

I must find an answer, if not for me and the other lycans, then for Esse. My little fairy will not stay wingless forever, as convenient as that would be. When her wings finally do come in, she is trapped.

From what Chiron has said, not every fairy can travel unseen on their wings the way he and Harlequin can. Should Esse's wings not contain enough reflective pigments in spectrums of green and blue, she would be easily seen from both the sky and the ground while flying. There is always the option to have a magus charm her with a branded rune that would cause the human eye to perceive her as something other than a tiny flying person with butterfly wings, but such methods are costly and often take a toll on the wearer of the runic brand.

Bottom line, if I cannot find us a way out of our situation before those wings appear, Esse's days are numbered. She might as well be mortal.

After about three minutes on the Gator moving at low speed over the uneven, narrow trail, we round the final curve that leads to the top of the glade. As the valley that forms the glade comes into view, I get my first glimpse at Esse's handy work. I stop the Gator, transfixed by all that two faeries can accomplish in one day.

"Would you look at that," I remark aloud to myself.

The two of them have completely altered the landscape. In one day they have managed to fully encircle the lake with trees, including three large willows, and create a natural rope swing over the surface of the lake. The pair have even fashioned six stone tables complete with shaped boulders draped in furs for seats.

Apples!

Kiro catches the scent of apples wafting up from below us.

I decided a canine compromise was in order, but we used your beloved pumpkins for the lake. I inform Kiro, amused at his childlike excitement.

"What do you think?" A familiar voice inquires from behind me. While lost in thought, Esse has materialized behind me, hovering slightly off the ground with a triumphant smile on her face.

"You did all of this!" I laugh, shaking my head in admiration of all their hard work.

"With some help of course." She nods her head indicating for me to turn around.

To my left, Chiron has landed as silently as an owl in the night. He smiles and gives the slightest wave of his hand.

They both certainly know how to sneak up on a guy. I notice.

"Good to see you Chiron. Sorry I have not been around much lately. You and Esse have done an amazing job with all of the preparations. Are you as excited as she is for this festival? I am sure Esse has told you all about it by now."

"I am just delighted we will not have to slaughter any goats for the modern version of this feast."

I stifle a laugh, leaning casually against the Gator. "Nope. No goats were harmed in the making of this festival. However, I make no promises regarding the safety of the rabbits living here."

Esse shoots me a cross look before fluttering over to sit gracefully on the back of the Gator.

She is tired. Kiro observes.

Upon closer inspection, Esse does appear to be more worn out than usual. Her exhaustion should come as no surprise. Though growing up a small forest overnight was once child's play for her, losing the Great Tree that fueled her power left Esse permanently depleted. Additionally, the loss of three of the four Great Trees has left all faeries severely compromised. Esse's body now responds violently to iron; should the metal even touch her skin, it would leave a bubbling mark behind.

43

"Did the two of you seriously grow an apple tree?" I ask them, trying to take my mind off the grim reality now faced by the entire fairy race, the love of my life included.

"We grew three actually." Chiron boasts with a proud smile. "We should be able to get the apples we need to fill the targets from these three trees. We also decided to mix the apples in with the pumpkins in the lake."

"Excellent." I turn my attention to Esse. "I do not suppose you have plans for lunch?"

"I am starving. Do you mind if we take a break for lunch Chiron?"

"Not at all. I could use a bit of rest anyway." Chiron assures her.

She flashes her second a grateful smile. Adjusting to balancing a life here with me while maintaining her close friendship with Chiron has not been a simple task.

The Order better hope that we fae never find our way into the light of day. Should the day ever come when we no longer need to hide to stay alive, I will make it my mission to burn them all to the ground, not just for what they have done to us but to their own kind.

The Order lent its power of influence to the Catholic faith at a time when the faith was still fragile and small. What the Catholic church thought was a symbiotic relationship quickly became parasitic until the Order, whose true motives were nearly brought into the light, retreated and became but a myth to most Catholics. These days, the Order is regarded amongst the Catholic faith as the Illuminati is regarded amongst historians. But to we fae, the Order is a very real and present danger.

Like wolves among sheep, they hide their actions by donning the cross and traditional attire of the church. Many Order members even hold high standing amongst the church as bishops and even archbishops.

Exploiting the powers and lives of fae, that is one thing; it is easy to understand how humans could do such a thing out of fear. But, to exploit the faith of innocent people, is unforgivable. I muse bitterly. Considering the sheer number of lives ruined by the actions of a few power-hungry humans puts both Kiro and me in a foul mood.

"I am sure Esse will be back here tomorrow. And, Chiron, you know you are always welcome up at the manor. You don't even need to hide your wings once you are inside; our security is top-notch." I remind the weary fairy, hoping to take my mind off the atrocities of the world.

Chiron smiles at us, a warm and genuine expression that, for a brief moment, fills me with hope. "I appreciate everything that you have done for us Kal. Now, go eat while you have the chance."

Chiron makes his way, on foot, down the slope to his cabin below, clearly conserving energy. I restart the engine in the Gator and turn the vehicle back toward home.

"You are both being careful about the flying and the fairy magic, right?" I verify. "You know what would happen if some punk with a camera phone saw you or even a low passing plane or drone."

"Kal." Before she speaks another word, I know that Ellesse is upset. "You of all creatures should know better than to tell me such things. I know better than anyone the price to be paid for being seen. However, I refuse to stop living my life. A life spent in a cage is, whether physical or self-imposed, is not a life at all. I refuse to fear the very part of me that makes me special." She declares.

"You are right, of course. Just promise me again that you will be careful. Please." Begging is not something I am accustomed to doing, but if it will get my little fairy to be careful, I am all for it.

Force would never work. Kiro thinks to himself analytically, wanting only, in his way, to keep her safe.

The thought of using force to make Esse do anything, even for her safety, sickens me.

45

I would never allow the situation to come to violence or brute strength. Besides, she has her trump card. I remind Kiro.

"I promise," Ellesse grumbles bitterly.

Before I can think of a more pleasant topic to discuss, my phone vibrates in my jacket pocket. Esse, who takes immediate notice of the buzzing, fishes in my pocket for the source of the intrusion.

"Esse..."

"Keep driving. Are you not the one who told me not to use these little devices while operating a motorized vehicle? Worry about your own machine."

"All-terrain vehicles do not count. I was referring more to cars and I can stop the Gator you know. No texting while driving applies to you too little fairy." I retort, resisting Esse's attempts to retrieve my phone.

"I do not drive." She answers simply, finally succeeding in acquiring my cell phone.

I cannot get her to use the cell phone I bought her, but she has no issue with using mine.

We spoil her. Kiro asserts half-jokingly.

"Esse," I growl again, attempting to convey the urgency in keeping my business private without offending the female I love most in the world.

"Relax grumpy wolf," Esse murmurs placing her chin on my shoulder lightly. "The message makes no sense to me anyway."

"We absolutely must discuss the meaning of the term *invasion of privacy.*" I sigh, knowing I have lost this battle. "Read it to me, quietly."

Pressing her lips to my ear Esse recites the message to me. "Old Mill Brewery. 8:15 pm, the tenth." Esse pauses, puzzled by the message for a moment but clever enough to guess the meaning. "Does that make sense? Is this something to do with Feng?"

"Yes, the message denotes the location, date, and time for our meeting with Feng. The good news is that the location is perfect. You will be able to stay close enough to be informed of everything happening without ever being in danger. As a precaution, your scent will be masked beforehand."

She nods in agreement. "Will you be safe?" she asks cautiously.

"It is not smart to distract the driver." I point out in an attempt to lighten the mood. Though I do care for my safety, I care more about Esse's life.

"You said the Gator does not count. Kal, you cannot ask me to make promises regarding my safety without also taking steps to assure your safety." She points out, eternally too clever for her own good.

She is always right. Kiro smirks cleverly in the back of my mind.

"I promise I will do everything in my power to remain safe. Though I will not deny you are my priority and nothing short of death with change that." I try not to sound too rigid, not wanting Esse to feel as though I have devalued her feelings.

"Then it is a damn good thing that you are my priority. With both of us prioritizing one another we should be prepared for anything." She declares enthusiastically.

How can someone whose entire existence hangs by a thread be so overwhelmingly optimistic? Of all the creatures in this world, Esse has more reason than any to be a cynic to the core. If only I could have just an ounce of her optimism. It is times like this, when my little fairy serves as the singular spot of brightness in my ever-darkening world, that I realize how much I need her in my life.

The manor slowly comes into view through the tall grass and well-trimmed shrubbery. As the historic, yet elegantly rebuilt, dwelling draws ever closer, the structure brings with it the promise of food and pleasant, unimportant conversation.

I have loved the historic manor since the day it came into Don's possession, though it was covered in ivy and falling apart back then. Over the course of a decade, we had the old castle repaired with as much historic accuracy as we could manage. According to Don, the manor, formerly the castle of a wealthy landowner during the 1500s, is a hybrid structure that started as a tower house and was gradually added to and modernized over time. Though it resembles a castle in some ways, its architecture and fortifications have all been completely modernized. After coming into my possession, Red and I added several modern amenities such as the twelve-car garage with a full lift, the solar paneling, and the greenhouse outback.

I pull up to the front door and let Esse off the Gator so that she can get lunch ready while I put the tiny vehicle away. I decide to send the information regarding the meeting location and time to Red to distribute to the others. With the tenth only being five days from now, I will need everyone working to be ready for what is to come immediately.

I had not expected this rogue prime to respond so soon. Truthfully, I was not sure that he would agree to meet at all. All signs thus far point to the man being incredibly unstable.

Planning for so many contingencies...we have our hands full on this one, especially the twins.

With the harbinger of our impending doom sent to Red to relay, I make my way to the manor kitchen for, a no doubt meat-free, lunch.

Plants are gross. Kiro complains.

Do not complain. I do not complain when you eat freshly killed rabbits or squirrels. We do share a stomach.

Hurry up, slowpokes! A new voice breaks through our conversation.

We are coming, Esse. I assure my impatient fairy as we close the front door behind us. Though I can make out basic sentences from Esse through telepathic communication, conversing in such a manner still falls, primarily, to Kiro. As a wolf, he can communicate with our little fairy with relative ease.

I hurry to the dining room and take my usual seat beside Esse. Despite Kiro's resistance to all things green, we waste no time in scarfing down our salad. Esse sits patiently, after somehow finishing before me, and waits for me to finish my lunch. I had not realized how hungry I was until I was presented with food.

Finally, Esse speaks. "So what did you do after India?"

Her abrupt question catches me off guard. "Is that where we left off?" I inquire surprised at the efficiency of her memory.

"Most definitely." Esse nods eagerly, her bright, gem-like eyes fixed on me like the eyes of a hungry cat.

"Well it has been a while, and my memory is not as sharp as yours, but I believe after India we headed to China. That is where I honed most of my fighting skills."

"I thought you learned how to fight in Europe," Esse interjects.

"Only with weapons. Europeans of that day were not known for hand-to-hand combat." I clarify.

"Tell me again when the man made electricity? Why did he not harness the power of the storms and sun the way we do? It seems to me that he made it unnecessarily difficult for himself." Esse interjects curiously.

"Humans, for all their knowledge, are not as smart as they believe themselves to be," I explain. "In all fairness, humans do not know the versatility of energy. Their bodies do not harness, create, or process energy the way our bodies do. That is why even witches do not always show an aptitude for certain magics. The human body has evolved in a way that they no longer possess functional mani, or what they would call chakras."

"I thought chakras were only in the spine," Esse interjects.

"In the mind of most humans, yes, they are. In spiritual reality, the chakra points in the spine form the main gates for energy flow through networks that no longer exist in the human body. So, in a way, chakras are only in the spine for humans."

"Where did you learn about all of this chakra stuff?" Esse asks mystified.

"In India of course!" I laugh. "It is all just different ways of saying the same thing."

"So, India taught you chakras and China taught you how to fight. Where did you go next?" Esse asks, getting ahead of herself in her quest to see the world as I have seen it.

"After China, I spent some time backtracking. Several decades were passed here in Europe until Don brought me another whisper of a valuable artifact rumored to be residing on the one content I had been dying to see. By that time, planes had become a secure means of travel, though they were much smaller than the one you flew on. I traveled by plane to Africa. That is where I met Andre, my third ally in this fight to change the fate of our people. Although, he went by a different name back then."

"Andre...that is Sela's partner! I get to meet them both soon!" She declares excitedly.

"Yes, and you will also meet their alpha, Carlos." I remind her.

"So, Carlos is the alpha of their pack because his father is dead?" Esse probes cautiously.

"Yes and no. He and his brothers, most of them anyway, are not like the other primes. They are certainly not like Feng. Carlos' brother killed their father for control of the pack and, for reasons he has never disclosed, Carlos then usurped his brother and seized control of the Brazilian territory. Since then, Carlos has united the lower packs of his territory into an organized chain rather than warring clusters of cartel goons."

"It does not bother you that Carlos has never mentioned why he took control?" Esse raises a worried eyebrow at me.

I shrug casually, flashing the worried fairy my most reassuring smile. "Some people do not like talking about their pain."

Esse's eyes darken with an all too familiar shadow, a look of pain I know all too well.

"I understand." She nods.

Esse rises and picks up her plate. "Kal, the date from the phone, when is it?" she asks.

"Five days from now, technically four since the day is more than half over now," I respond, raising my head toward her as I lean back in my chair.

"Good." She leans in dangerously close to me, her delicate lips brushing my forehead. "Then the family will not mind if I borrow you for the rest of the day."

She gently kisses the top of my head with a feather-light touch, then takes my empty plate from in front of me and strides away toward the kitchen as light as air itself.

Gods, I love her.

Four

"Annie's report is flawless and Dex has eyes on us from every angle as well as eyes on every door. We have enough bullets to kill a small army and those men Ivan sent are almost as accurate as Annie with those rifles we tested. Just make sure to keep your cloak on and your head low. The cloak will keep your scent hidden and as long as you stay out of sight no one will know that you are here."

Who are you trying to convince? Kiro jabs at me mentally in an odd attempt at livening the mood in our mind without breaking his focus.

Kiro, as usual, is correct in his assessment of my chaotic mental state. Even I am unsure of whether I am convincing Esse or myself.

"We have been over this nearly a dozen times Kal. Everything will be fine, Doc said so herself. We survived the Order; we will survive this as well." For good measure, Esse takes my hand and squeezes it reassuringly.

"Doc's vision cannot account for the fluidity of time, you know that. Just take care not to use magic of any kind. Maintaining your anonymity is imperative. If anything should go sideways today, just sit tight and make for this car as soon as it is safe to do so. The backup phone is in the glovebox. The first number saved on the phone is Don, though it will not be marked with his name. Call that number if I do not appear at the car within three minutes and follow Don's instructions exactly. Doc has instructions to flee with you as well if anything goes wrong. Do you have any questions?" I recite the jumbled laundry list in my head as clearly as possible.

"Nothing is going to happen." Esse asserts with perfect certainty.

Before I can argue further, Annie's voice sounds in my ear through the earpiece Dex gave me before getting into the car.

"It's done. All is quiet here."

She knows, as they all do, to speak under the assumption that we are being listened to. I click the call button on the hand-held radio twice in rapid succession, my way of confirming she has been heard.

The abandoned brewery comes into focus through the windshield of the car. Several smaller wooden buildings, mostly for storage, surround the massive brick structure which houses the primary brewing facility. This once functional brewery was previously owned and operated by none other than Don Drafe, the mysterious man behind the curtain.

Though even I know little of Don's background, his motivations have always been plain for all to see. For reasons unknown, Don holds a furious grudge against the Order. He has dedicated most of his long life to amassing a modest fortune to fund his various projects. No one knows exactly who Don is or how much wealth he has amassed, but he has been a faithful ally in the fight to unite the lycanthrope race against a common adversary.

With the blueprints provided by Don to the twins, we were able to carefully plan for every eventuality in preparation for today's rendezvous. Annie spent all of yesterday pouring over the blueprints and each of her numerous contingencies with each one of us individually until we could recite the information back to her flawlessly. Should any of us be separated from the rest, we each know exactly what to do to make it safely out of the Old Mill and back to the manor or one of Don's safehouses.

All that is left to do now is ensure Esse is ready to go.

"Stop the car Red," I instruct from my position directly behind the driver's seat.

I extend my hand to Esse. Resting in the center of my palm is a tiny earpiece, identical to my own.

"Put this in your ear. I know you hate things near your ears, but it will allow you to hear everything that is happening inside the main building." I explain.

Next, I fish a second radio from my pocket and hand it to her. To prevent feedback, we decided to use the earpieces in

53

conjunction with the handhelds to communicate with one another. I hand Esse the radio and explain how it works to her.

"Press this tiny button three times rapidly if you need something but only if it is urgent."

"Why can I not speak to Kiro if something is wrong?" She asks worriedly, her thin eyebrows furrowing in dismay.

"Kiro will be occupied. He will need to keep a close eye on everything inside and outside of the building as well as the surrounding buildings. This requires constant focus using my sense of smell, hearing, and sight without taking away from my mental focus. Splitting the conscious mind this way is taxing on us both. If you attempt to contact either of us, Kiro may lose focus altogether. Feng may be waiting for just such a situation. However, you should not need to contact us during the meeting. If all goes well it will be quick and to the point and we will be home in time for a late lunch." I attempt to make my voice as reassuring as possible, but Esse's face betrays her concern.

"Where will I be?" She asks softly.

"You see that tiny building just to the left of the main one?" I ask.

She nods.

"That's the one. You will be safely obscured toward the back of the crowded room. It is laid out so that if anyone enters the room besides one of us, you can knock over the nearest stack of crates and the rest will fall toward the door either barricading you inside or disabling the intruder."

"I will not need wind to knock them over?" She asks, her eyes widening slightly.

"Not at all," I assure her. "Remember, lycanthropes can sense the use of magic, even your wind-based abilities. One final thing; Red will be with you until you are situated."

"Why Red? Also, should Doc not stay with me? She has to hide too."

"Not a good idea. Having you and Doc together in the same place would leave everyone vulnerable, especially you and Doc. Both of you are using Red's scent to conceal yourself and bundles of clothing with his scent on them have also been placed in other buildings around the property to throw anyone nosing around off your trails. Doc will be close by, do not worry."

Esse pouts for a moment, looking as though she is fighting the urge to debate the matter with me.

"You promised." I remind her.

With a heavy sigh, Esse nods her agreement and turns to Red to let him know she is ready.

This will be over soon. I remind myself, suppressing the pang of anxiety rising inside me at the thought of being separated from Esse.

Red opens his door and exits the car, opening Esse's door to cover her exit from the car. Neither of them moves until Kiro has had a chance to clear the area, waiting patiently for the wind to shift once so he can properly survey the surrounding terrain.

All clear. He verifies.

With a nod to Red, he and Esse depart in the direction of the tiny building. I try not to think about the slim chance that this may be the last time I ever see her.

She is safe. Kiro asserts absent-mindedly.

That is what matters. I agree.

We will see her again. Kiro adds with more certainty as we exit the car to make our way inside.

Gus radios a final all-clear as I reach the door to the building, having swept the inside of the main building from top to bottom in search of any deception on the part of the startup prime. Despite Ireland being in late fall, the weather today is fairly warm with only a gentle breeze and partly cloudy sky.

What a perfect day for a bloodbath. I stew callously. *I would rather eat rabbit food for the rest of my life than be here right now.*

The absence of a witty remark from Kiro tells me that he is already fully focused on the task at hand. I push past the steel-framed door, taking care to shut it behind me. The room within is damp and cool, like a basement but with high ceilings rimmed in a balcony-style second floor with offices overlooking large vats and brewing equipment. The only discernable scents are those of Gus and Red.

As planned. Annie and Dex wearing Red's clothes, after taking cold showers, was an effective strategy. They did an excellent job concealing their scents as they swept the rooms and positioned the snipers and cameras. The cameras are barely visible to even Kiro's keen eyes. I note with pride. *There is no better team than my family.*

All that remains now is to wait. The team of six is hidden alongside Annie on the rooftops while Dex mans the monitors from a safe distance. Gus hovers behind me, his wolf on high alert. After thirty seconds or so of waiting Red appears from the doorway.

"Nothing yet." He confirms as I raise a questioning eyebrow. A nod of acknowledgment from the silent red-head tells me that Esse is well settled in her hiding place.

I turn to Gus who gives the same gesture, indicating Doc is safely tucked away as well. With a pang of guilt I realize that, for the first time since meeting Gus and Doc, I now know exactly how Gus felt the day he saw her for the first time.

How tempting it must have been for him to ignore his feelings and risk isolation and eternal loneliness to destroy the one thing he knew would make him vulnerable. The strength it took to completely change his nature in the span of a single heartbeat is beyond admirable.

The waiting ends abruptly as Dex radios in from his vantage point.

"Three cars approaching."

So he intends to make a show of this then. So be it. Such reckless tactics are typical of an unhinged individual. We are ready.

"Any indication on how many?"

"Full cars. Can't tell which one of them is him." Dex responds.

"No matter. Radio silence from here on."

Why do I get the feeling this Feng will be less than cooperative?

Sure enough, roughly a minute and a half later the pompous prime comes bursting through the door. The way he strides into the room as though he owns the place, with his too flashy, worn once, designer shoes and overly tight pants, makes me want to rip him into pieces on principal alone.

Has no one impressed upon you the concept of laying low and blending into the middle-class society? Is this man trying to get us all caught and put in cages like dogs?

While the flashy punk of a prime makes himself at home amongst the brewing equipment, his goons, which total nearly ten strong, begin fanning out to not-so-subtly snoop about the open floor of the room.

Not an experienced bunch. More brawn than brain for sure. I calculate.

Their scents are all over the place. Cannot tell one from another. Kiro grows restless in the presence of so many wolves, each coated in a mix of scents so interwoven they have formed a distinctly new smell.

Shit. With that many scents, they did not come to Ireland alone. The trip from the states takes at least a day and I am sure they landed long before now. These scents are too interwoven not to be fresh. Yet again, this wannabe prime has risked calling attention by traveling with so many men. I can only hope he did not fly commercial.

"What a dump, this *Ireland.* We will need to make this quick, I do not know how you Irish brutes tolerate such a dreary place. What a waste of an island." The flashy one, who had already distinguished himself as Feng by appearance alone, sneers with utter disdain.

"I am not Irish," I reply flatly.

"Just the carrot tops then?" He laughs moronically.

57

Neither Gus nor Red budges an inch. Ironically, Red is only about one-sixteenth Irish by blood, though he has heard every carrot top joke there is.

"I am, however, all for making this quick. I have far better things to be doing with my time." I continue, paying no mind to the shrimpy prime's laughter. "We primes live by laws meant to protect not only ourselves but all lycanthropes. We do not go turning humans at will and we stick to our turf unless otherwise instructed or a challenge is declared. I should feed you your larynx right here and now for showing your face uninvited on another prime's turf. That prime so happens to be an ally of mine, and he is none too pleased to be dealing with this inconvenience." I growl threateningly.

"Oh, I know all about you and your allies. Everyone thinks you are such a badass because you went and threw a tantrum that ended your daddy's pack."

Such ironic words coming from an overgrown pup.

"My pack stands here now, and my past is of no concern here. This meeting is concerned only with your actions. I will warn you only once; clean up your mess or I will do it for you. Believe me, you will not like how I clean things up."

Unfortunately for this welp, he has brought up the one subject that strikes a nerve in me, almost as much as threatening Esse would have.

Before either Feng or I can move, I hear three faint radio clicks from the earpiece.

She could be upset by what the flashy one has said. Kiro offers, suppressing blind, panic-driven, rage.

She would not do that. She promised us, remember; and she never breaks her word unless it is life or death. Let us not panic yet.

As though following a silent cue, Feng rises casually from his perch and takes two long, lightning-fast strides in my direction. Unfortunately for him, his actions are both predictable and sluggish. Kiro sees the attack coming long before the man reaches us.

"'Tis far enough!" Gus roars, stepping in front of me as I dodge the Chinese prime with ease.

Gus knocks the scrawny male back without giving an inch, using only one arm and the strength of his core. Feng halts his attack, his men bristling as they form an ill-advised circle around the three of us and their alpha.

"My *mess* is the least of your worries Greyback. Spineless primes like you are the real problem facing our people. You think you are so great and gifted, but you are the one who is making a mess of things." Feng snarls wickedly. "Who decided that humans get to run this world? While you fossils sit around, hiding in your holes, the human vermin grow more brazen by the day, consuming everything in their path. They have destroyed our way of life and still, you lot do nothing to stop them. I do not intend to wait around to die like a dog."

"The issues you speak of will be solved in due time, but they must be dealt with in the right way. Recklessness will only get us all killed." I chance a step closer to the prime, allowing Gus to pull back into his former position. Red has not moved an inch, completely unphased by the situation as expected. The rabid look in Feng's eyes and the cocky grin on his face finally push me beyond my point of break.

"My methods will not concern you much longer." Feng's grin broadens into a twisted smile of contempt.

Tik. Tik. Tik.

Three more clicks sound in my ear, this time much faster than the first three.

"Red."

Red nods knowingly, not requiring an explanation or further instruction from me. He heard the same three urgent clicks I heard and knows exactly what they mean.

I chance a glance at Gus from the corner of my left eye. Though I am sure he is trembling, both with rage and fear, inside, he does well in keeping such feelings to himself. One would never know that the most important thing in the world to Gus was, at this moment, in jeopardy.

As Red exits through the circle of goons, not a single one moves to stop him. On the contrary, the circle parts like the Red Sea. For all his silent charm, Red's aura can portray a ruthless intent that would bring most unseasoned lycans to their knees in close range. The moment Red pulls open the door Kiro tenses in the back of my mind.

Lycans. In wolf form. At least ten.

Shit. The reckless son of a...

Feng moves toward me again, this time with near blinding speed. Despite the increase in speed, his movements remain predictable and Gus easily counters him. This time, the mob of inexperienced brutes intervenes on Feng's behalf.

Good thing Gus is worth twice the number of these fools gathered here today. What can you see? I ask Kiro as I dodge poorly executed attacks from Feng's goons.

They move like pups. Reckless and disjointed. No communication.

Annie will have no problems dealing with the outside then. I confirm.

We go to her now. Kiro demands desperately.

Too risky. Focus on Feng first.

Reluctantly, Kiro shifts his focus to the task at hand, as do I. Red hesitates at the doorway, feeling compelled to assist us inside.

"Red go!" I instruct.

He obeys and I hit the com to give Annie the green light to fire upon the closing wolves.

"Hit it now Annie. Dex, keep sharp. I do not want a single wolf straying from this property in their animal body. I repeat, do not let them cross the damn property line!"

With my focus split, Feng redirects his attacks at me, his goons struggling to keep Gus occupied. If it were not for the close quarters, Gus could easily have outmaneuvered these novice fighters, each of whom lacks skill.

While Kiro keeps his focus on Feng's movements, allowing me to easily keep out of reach of the primes recklessly thrown fists and blurringly fast kicks, I listen in for Annie's little surprise. Two clicks come through in rapid succession on the earpieces and both Gus and I break away from the struggle to shield our eyes. Three remotely activated flash bombs detonate from the corners of the large room and four smoke canisters drop from the upper balcony.

Gus wastes no time. Seizing his opportunity to regain the upper hand, he launches at the nearest lycan, ripping the man's chest open like a barbarian. He moves rapidly from one stunned wolf to the next until they finally wise up and move into a formation to protect one another's backs.

A smart move but it will not save you. I pity the poor bastards who now stand no chance against the surprisingly agile Irishman. Under different circumstances, I would have preferred to settle this without spilling so much blood, but at times it seems bloodshed is unavoidable.

Before I can dwell on the horrors of war and the misfortune of our situation, Kiro interrupts. *I lost Feng.*

I do not bother attempting to see or smell through the smoke. Rather, I feel my way through, probing for the slightest trace of Feng's aura. When I finally locate the cowardly prime, he throws one of his men in my path in an underhanded attempt to flee. The unfortunate man is thin, almost scrawny, with no muscle to protect his weak points. I effortlessly grab the stranger by one arm, snapping the thin limb as easily as if it were a twig, then cast him to the side to be dealt with later.

The scrawny brown-haired man lets out a series of ear-splitting yowls. He evidently has never broken a single bone in his body; unlike Gus and me who have, between the two of us, broken nearly every bone in our bodies three times over. I shudder to think what our insides would look like on an x-ray.

By now, the sound of silenced rifle fire has filled the air outside the slightly cracked door.

Those men did not need to die. I observe vengefully. *Until a few weeks ago, I am sure most of them were humans who knew nothing of the struggles of being a lycanthrope. I am certain none of them thought for a moment that they would die like this.*

"This is on you," I growl into the billowing cloud of smoke that fills the cold metal interior of the brewery. "Those men out there did not have to die like animals. The lycans who chose to follow you in your ill-advised quest for blood did not have to lose their lives like this. *You* did this! We could have faced the threat of humanity as a united front, instead, you have only served to reduce our strength and blame your shortcomings on me. We lycans will never accomplish anything so long as we continue to fight amongst ourselves like children. Brute force will never be enough to stand against the militaries of more than three hundred organized, well-armed, countries. You have made your last mistake, you spoiled welp. Now you will pay for such wastefulness with your life, Feng."

As the smoke begins to clear, I hear Annie breach the hatch in the ceiling above. She comes in hot, pistols blazing like a true western gunslinger. The acrid stench of blood mixes with the already metallic smell of the room's machinery. Such smells in combination with the gradually dissipating gunfire outside only agitate Kiro further.

She is not safe! We go now! The flashy one is not even here. Kiro insists, almost violently, struggling to resist the urge to move my body using his own will.

Running to her now would only draw attention to her location. You know full well that we would sense her pain if she were hurt. We stay put and find the weasel that started all of this.

Without giving Kiro a choice, I advance slowly through the fading wisps of smoke. I search the faces of each dead lycanthrope I encounter on the floor, hoping that one might be Feng. All the while, I carefully scan each corner and under each piece of equipment, refusing to let my guard down until I am sure Feng has fled the building.

Even a cornered rat can be dangerous under the right circumstances.

A guttural howl to my right halts my advance, drawing both my attention as well as Kiro's.

"Gus!" Annie cries. "Kal, he is down!"

I hurry around the vat to my right and find Annie standing over Gus, scanning the area behind the vats for any sign of life. The friendly giant is laying in a pool of blood, luckily not all his, holding his right side with both arms.

"The slippery little fella slipped into wolf form and bit me," Gus growls through gritted teeth.

"Can you stand Gus?" I ask, stooping down slightly to examine his injuries.

"Aye. Stop fussin' lad. Don't you even think of calling her here."

"I know better than that, old friend," I assure him.

Dex's static-filled voice interrupts our conversation through the earpieces. "Is Feng down?"

"Kiro insists that he is gone. Tell me those wolves outside did not scatter."

"I lost sight of three though only one was close enough to the property line to have gotten away. More than likely we will find the other two on the property hiding or dead." Dex informs me regretfully.

Red appears looking somewhat disheveled.

Kiro bristles like an angry porcupine. *Why is he not with her?*

"Red, where is she?"

"She is fine, but things became complicated," Red explains, leaving out crucial details as usual.

I have not the patience to ask for more information from him. Kiro is now clawing at the inside of my mind like a rabid animal caught in a snare. There is no longer any pacifying him; the thought of anything happening to Esse has worked him into a frenzy.

Try to control yourself. I may need you.

Kiro offers no response but stops fighting just the same. Without needing Kiro to pilot my body, I rush for the door, recoiling as the outside air hits my sensitive nose. The pungent mix of metallic blood and gun powder is overwhelmingly thick. In three short heartbeats, we have already reached the door to Esse's building. Alarm bells sound in my head immediately.

A dark blood trail leads from one side of the tiny building into the now open doorway. Inside everything is still standing just as I left it before bringing Esse to the property.

Why did she not do as I instructed? I wonder in fearful frustration.

The blood trail continues down the side of the narrow corridor that leads to the back corner of the building. Bloody handprints mar the weathered walls of the wooden interior.

This blood is too dark to be hers. I assure Kiro, whose anxiety is now affecting my breathing.

"Kal?"

That is her voice.

I believe I know Ellesse's voice by now Kiro. Please calm yourself before our heart explodes.

"Are you alright? Is there someone else here?" I ask her carefully steadying my voice.

"I am fine. I need you over here though." She calls back to me softly.

I push my way deliberately through the overstuffed building, strategically avoiding the load-bearing crates. Though I still cannot see our little fairy, the presence of her aura grows faintly the closer we move to her through the storage facility. After painstakingly pushing our way to the back of the building, Esse's disguised scent becomes distinguishable amidst Red's scent and the stench of blood.

"Kal!" she calls again, more urgently, as we close in on her location.

"I am nearly there. Esse, this blood trail...are you certain no one else is here with you?"

"You will see when you get here." She answers calmly, with no trace of nervousness.

This does not bode well. However, she does not sound as though she has been coerced.

Just move! Hurry! Kiro has lost all concern for our safety, a temperament he has never displayed before in his centuries of existence, aside from the day we nearly perished in the Canadian woods.

I round the corner and find myself met with a scene out of a horror film. Broken crates and barrels clutter the floor, crunching and cracking underfoot as we step over shattered glass and shards of metal from barrel bindings. The blood trail ends abruptly amidst the chaos.

"Took you long enough!" Esse's frantic voice draws my attention to where she has huddled herself into the far corner. Frustration is etched into every line of her delicate face. "Is it safe to use magic now?"

"Why would you need to use magic?" I move closer to examine her, unsettled by her flustered appearance and the unexplained blood trail.

"Kal hurry. I need your help here. He is not getting any less injured. I thought lycanthropes healed quickly. I wish I had thought to learn more about lycan anatomy." She trips over her words in apparent frustration.

"Esse...what do you mean he?"

I push the final broken crate aside, revealing a nearly dead male lycan lying in a pool of blood in front of Esse. The unfortunate creature appears to have been shot in the chest, partially damaging his heart. With his heart damaged to such an extent, the wolf is now unable to heal or transition back into a human body.

"Esse." I attempt to keep my voice calm and even. "Would you care to explain what is happening here?"

"He is hurt, that is what is happening here. This poor wolf just stumbled in here and started...I do not know how to describe it.

I think he was trying to get back into his human body. You can see how well that worked out. He passed out and now he is back here slowly bleeding to death. I patched up the tiny scratches as best I could without leaving the building or using magic, but he needs magic...he needs Doc too. Where is she?"

"Esse you should not have healed him at all. Especially without me here." I scold the reckless fairy.

"Red was here." She protests, not bothering to glance up at me. Esse remains focused busily on the task before her. Without waiting on my approval she starts pulling water out of the air to use for healing the damage to the wolf's heart. However, with the moon nowhere near risen, and no understanding of gunshot wounds, her progress is slow at best.

No. Kiro snarls in my head, as much to Esse as to me. *Let the mutt die.*

"Kiro!" Esse throws a horrified look over her shoulder. "This creature is a living thing. All life is sacred. We may have been forced to shoot him, but that does not mean we have the right to leave him for dead. If the gods wanted him dead, he would have died the instant the bullet pierced his chest."

Well? I probe Kiro for a response.

She is right. He relents bitterly, though he is far from happy.

I let out a sigh, feeling both relieved and concerned. "For starters, your magic will not be enough until we get the bullet out. Without the presence of the moon, you should conserve your energy to put toward other healing methods, such as fastening some natural means of repairing the damaged arteries."

"I do not understand. Bullets have never stopped you from healing?" She protests.

"We use silver bullets that split on impact to slow the healing of the lycans we shoot. The silver will not kill the lycan as it does in Hollywood movies, but the substance slows down our healing ability."

"Like iron?" She interjects, her voice wrought with disgust.

"Yes," I admit reluctantly. "Like iron."

"How could you use methods like this? How is this any better than what they did?" She hisses, still focused on the tawny furred wolf in front of her.

"Esse..."

"How do we remove it?" she gives me no opportunity to defend my methods, not that I could defend them to her. Like it or not, Esse is accurate in her assessment. Just as the Order would argue that their ends justify the means, I have made the same argument in this situation.

"We need a blade," I mumble, running a bloody hand through my disheveled hair. "And we will need a means of keeping him unconscious."

"I can do the second one. We need Doc." She reasserts.

I radio Red.

"Red, we need Doc. Whenever you and Doc finish with Gus please rush over to the secondary stash house."

"Alright." Red answers simply.

"Do you think he will ever speak more?" Esse asks, trying to distract herself.

"I doubt it," I reply, grateful for the out.

With Feng still on the loose, and Esse insistent upon putting herself at risk, I decide to cover our bases and be certain that Feng has retreated.

"Annie, go ahead and regroup with Dex. Let us see if we can get eyes on Feng's retreat. And keep an ear out for any reports of wolves in the area around the brewery."

"Roger," Annie replies quickly.

Reckless. Kiro chimes in, only adding to my fears.

You have made your objections known. Do you want her to hate us?

"What is taking Red so long?" Esse frets. Her aura is suffocatingly tense, setting Kiro further on edge.

"Try to relax, Esse. He is coming. To put down a lycanthrope requires more than sixty percent damage to the heart. From what I can sense, his heart is still mostly functional, and he is a very fresh lycanthrope. That means he can hold on despite the blood loss."

"How much blood can one lycan lose?"

"Quite a bit. Around a third of their body's worth."

Esse turns to me in surprise. Blood loss is not a familiar concept among faeries as very few weapons can damage their bodies enough to cause extensive blood loss.

"The way that you speak implies that this lycanthrope is a lot younger than us. How do you know?" She asks curiously, turning her watchful gaze back to the ragged creature in front of her.

"Well, he is a former human. Based on his scent he was very recently turned. I would say a few months at most which is why he and his wolf were unable to come to terms and quell their panic when they were injured in the wolf's body." I explain slowly.

"That nose of yours never ceases to amaze me." Esse finally sounds a bit more like her gleeful self.

Red finally emerges from the still acrid-smelling brewery grounds outside the tiny building. Doc follows close behind him, her hoodie still pulled tight over her face.

"Let us take a look here." Doc smiles at Esse as she removes her hood and fishes in her medkit for a scalpel and some disinfectant.

"Does he really need that chemical stuff?" Esse asks raising an eyebrow at the healer.

"Honestly, it is just a precaution given the nature of his…unique genetic structure. The chemicals used are not like the ones you have experienced. These only target bacteria." Doc assures Esse.

"Kal said he will need to be kept unconscious?"

"Yes. I have no anesthetic; do you think you could manage to keep him out cold with that lulling thing you do?" Doc asks.

Esse nods. "How long?"

"About two minutes give or take thirty seconds depending upon the number of bullet fragments. Thankfully, crude surgery is effective on lycanthropes."

The two females begin the arduous task of repairing the damaged wolf. After a minute and a half, Esse's mani begin to glow the bright green color that indicates exhaustion.

She never used to tire like this. Kiro observes, feeding off of my own growing concerns.

"Just a bit longer," I assure Esse, trying not to let my personal feelings affect my voice or aura.

A few tense heartbeats later, Doc is finished.

"You can rest now; we are done. He should pull through just fine thanks to you." Doc smiles kindly at a now panting Esse as my little fairy pulls her shaking hands away from the wolf's still head.

"How is the cleanup and containment going out there?" I turn my attention to Red, attempting to dispel my worried thoughts on the matter of Esse's condition.

"The twins have their ears to the scanner and the Russians are working on cleanup for us." Red brings me up to speed.

"Good. Stay on top of the situation while I deal with this."

"Then you do not mind if I return to him?" Doc asks, clearly distraught over Gus' injuries.

"Of course; just stay concealed just in case." I remind her.

Doc finishes cleaning her tools and carefully repacks them before putting her hoodie back on. She rises quickly and follows Red, presumably, back to the main building.

"Deal with this how?" Esse asks, gritting her teeth slightly in clear distaste. Her posture suggests that convincing the agitated little fairy to see the risk incurred in this situation will be difficult.

"We know nothing about this man. He could be dangerous."

"We are not killing him and not leaving him to die. Especially after everything we just went through to save his life." Esse interjects, drawing her line in the sand before I can object.

"What do you propose?" I muse, attempting to avoid an argument that I will ultimately lose regardless of the outcome.

"We take him with us." She suggests.

"As a wolf? Esse that suggestion is incredibly dangerous. If he is seen in our car questions will be asked and the authorities will get involved."

"Kal you do not understand. This wolf is just like me." Esse sighs, looking down at the unlucky creature, now rapidly healing, with a mix of sorrow and ferocity that leaves me feeling more than a bit defensive.

"Explain." I coax flatly.

"He had a life before Feng came along and stole it away from him. This poor man may not have even been given the option to choose. At least I was afforded a choice in the end. Even if this man was given the option of joining Feng, I am sure no one gave him the whole story. Who is to say if he knew that he would be thrown into a civil war or face death at the hands of an order of fearful humans? When I was born the guardian, my choice was made for me, just as it was made for this man. Kal, you gave me a second choice, now I must give him one."

"Esse."

I do not have the heart to tell her how easily humans are persuaded to fill out the ranks of start-up packs such as Feng's. Promise them power, wealth, or immortality and most humans will gladly sell their souls. I have not the heart to tell her that this wolf she has cared for so fiercely likely chose this fate.

Would not matter now. Kiro growls.

That is true. Her mind is made up and nothing will change it. I agree.

No. He is waking up.

Sure enough, the young wolf begins to stir. With a series of tiny cracks and pops, his bone structure sets to altering itself back into that of a human male. I rush to remove my jacket and throw it over the soon to be naked man.

He has caused me enough trouble today, no way in hell I am letting Esse see him like that.

Insecure.

Kiro has returned to his more relaxed demeanor now that the immediate threat has passed. Sarcastic comments aside, Kiro's words do hold some truth. There are many days that I find myself wondering how different life would have been if I had only stumbled into that Canadian forest sooner. Three hundred years ago I still healed as quickly as the young lycan rapidly recovering on the dusty concrete floor. Two hundred years ago I had half the scars that mar my body and face. Over the centuries it seems that I have only accumulated more demons, both inside and out, than I care to admit. Though Esse would never say so, I know my nature and my checkered past bother her sometimes.

The young man's eyes finally flutter open revealing bright blue irises and a blank, groggy expression. I grab Esse protectively and pull the hood of her cloak over her head, earning a sour expression from the hot-tempered fairy.

If he has not seen her, then there is a chance we can resolve this peacefully and everyone can go home happy.

For several tense heartbeats, the man remains still, his eyes open but blank. Slowly, life begins to fill his eyes and he begins to look around. For a moment, his eyes and posture are calm but panic sets in rapidly driving the inexperienced lycan's mind to split once more into a chaotic state, caught between his human self and his wolf. Unlike those of us who were born this way, turned humans lack the mental fortitude to balance the two distinctly varied personalities in their minds. Surprisingly, the young man recovers quickly, opening his mouth to speak.

"Where am I?" he stammers fearfully, his eyes still flickering between us and his surroundings.

His wolf is non-aggressive but fearful. The human appears oddly calm. A warrior?

71

Possibly a former soldier from the states. I concur.

"Take it easy. As long as you move slowly and do not try anything stupid, you are perfectly safe here. You were shot but we repaired you."

Kiro keeps a watchful eye on the man's vitals and his aura, which remains an open book given his lack of training. The man's rapid breathing begins to slow, and his agitated wolf ceases his struggling.

"Thank you for that. For not letting me die I mean. The fact that you saved me must mean you either need something from me or you are not quite the monster we were told you are. Apparently, a lot of what they told us was less than accurate." The young man speaks slowly and with caution, as though worried he might say too much. "My name is Sam by the way."

"Alright Sam, I need you to answer a few questions for me."

Sam eyes me suspiciously but nods in reluctant agreement.

"Firstly, how did you find yourself mixed up in all of this? Where did you come from?" I probe.

"Well." Sam hesitates his body tensing and his aura swirling with an edge of fearful resistance.

Pay careful attention in case this Sam tries to pull one over on us.

Always careful. Kiro huffs indignantly.

Kiro makes a fair point. I have never known a single soul to tell a lie in Kiro's presence that the sly wolf could not detect.

"I am from the states, but there are a lot like me from all over the place. Rather, there *were* a lot like me."

Truth.

This will be a pain then. These people came from multiple countries; tracking them down and resolving their disappearances one by one will take precious time that we do not have. We will need to call Don.

"As for how I got here…" The young Sam trails off, his eyes clouding over.

"I realize your story might be difficult to tell and that you may even be worried for your family. I assure you, no harm will come to you so long as you answer my questions truthfully. You must explain to me exactly how this came to be."

"You misunderstand. I have no family to speak of. I was barely able to afford my apartment before…well, I do not remember much at first. I remember walking home one night like I always do after my graveyard shift, and this massive dog, or what I thought was a dog, jumped me. After that everything goes blank. The next thing I remember was waking up with all of my injuries healed and a splitting headache. I thought maybe I had dreamed it all, but I was not in my apartment." Sam explains carefully.

"Where were you when you woke up?"

Sam shakes his head. "I do not know. The room was small and damp and made of metal. I could smell the ocean. That's when I heard it."

"It?" I question.

"The voice in my head. I thought I was losing my mind."

"You mean your wolf?" I raise a questioning eyebrow at him.

"I guess. You have to believe me; I do not understand how any of this works or what has happened to me. I just do what they tell me."

"You keep saying they. They who?" I press.

"Feng and his henchmen. The ones who were supposed to be in the cars with him."

"I see. Continue; we need to know more about what happened to you. Every detail helps."

"For days they kept me locked up in that room. They barely fed me or let me sleep and there was no sun to tell the time of day. I began to think I would die and the voice in my head started freaking out like a rabid animal."

"No one explained anything to you about what was happening to you physically or mentally?" I can feel Esse tense behind me. Sam's story is understandably upsetting to her.

"Explain this? No. Believe me, questions were not met with kindness, so I stopped giving the situation much thought. Honestly, for a few days or so I believed I was dead and in hell. Then they finally opened the door and I realized I was very much alive, though I soon wished I were dead. The men who came through the door threw a bag over my head and shoved me in a car. Things grew worse from there. We were not permitted to speak much amongst ourselves, not that any of us were in talking moods." Sam stops talking abruptly. The memory of his ordeal starts to take its toll on him.

"That is alright, I have been around long enough to know what came next," I inform the young man.

Esse's questioning gaze burns two piercing holes through my back. I bite my lip hoping she has the good sense to remain silent until we have learned more.

"I understand the severity of your situation. However, I need your address and the contact information for anyone who may have reported you missing."

"What is going to happen to me?" Sam asks, his voice lacking even the slightest trace of nervousness. Despite his steady voice, his aura betrays his true feelings.

Before I can answer the brave lycanthrope, Esse clutches my arm. I stifle a warning growl knowing the price incurred for growling at her.

"Give me a moment Sam. Do not leave this spot."

Sam swallows hard but does not move as I assist Esse in rising to her feet. I keep myself carefully positioned between her and Sam as we make our way outside. We keep walking until I am certain that Sam cannot hear us, my eyes remaining fixed on the only exit to the tiny storage building.

"We are taking him with us," Esse states plainly, crossing her arms in overt defiance.

"There are risks." I protest.

"Kal."

"This is a very delicate situation."

"Kal."

"Feng could come looking for him. The Order might already be looking for Feng because of Sam's missing person report or any of the other individuals that Feng turned."

"You mean the dead ones." She purses her lips in frustration, her aura suggesting that she is perilously close to feeling outright anger.

"He is a missing person. All of them are." I groan.

"Were." She corrects me.

Looks like we are taking home another stray.

Five

"Sam, hurry up with the targets. How long does it take to stuff some apples into burlap?" Esse yells excitedly from the overgrown field she has made for our scavenger hunt. With the guests arriving any minute for the start of the three-night festival, Esse has taken to barking orders left and right in a frenzy. She is bound and determined to make everything perfect for our coalition's first Fall Moon Feast.

I must admit, I could not have done all of this without Esse.

She has taken care of all the decorations: fruit-filled pinatas and stationary targets for axes and arrows, pumpkins and apples floated in the lake, a field of tall grass stocked with lightly buried dried meats for scavenger hunting, and large stone tables with fall-themed centerpieces for the dinners. Esse even constructed a sparring ring, despite her distaste for all forms of violence.

"I am working as fast as I can! I am still tired from hauling pumpkins back and forth all morning!" Sam laughs, though he is still panting from his perch atop the wooden ladder.

"He is fitting in well, that Sam," I remark to no one in particular, still waiting for the other shoe to drop after the debacle with Feng.

Too close. Kiro complains, agitated by the growing friendship between Sam and Esse.

He would not dare. I assure my grumpy wolf. *Besides, she saved him, gave him a new life with a new sense of purpose. He feels indebted to her. After all, we would have let him die.*

He can get his own fairy. Kiro insists.

Now you know how she feels when we are too busy for her. I assert, knowing full well that the real reason behind Kiro's possessive behavior is the lack of free time he has had to spend with Esse.

Kiro remains silent though I can feel him brooding in the back of my mind. The intensity of his dark aura hangs over me like a heavy storm cloud just waiting to release a deluge of torrential rain and terrifying thunder upon me. For the time being, I resign myself to letting the stubborn creature brood.

I am sure the festivities lined up for tomorrow will cheer you right up.

Do not count on it. Kiro sulks.

"Kal, do you think the field is tall enough?" Esse calls back to me, not bothering to look up or even turn around.

"The field is perfect, little fairy," I assure her, still in awe of how much two determined faeries with only a quarter of their true power can accomplish in three weeks.

"In any case," I continue. "Carlos will be here in less than half an hour, so the field will have to do my little perfectionist."

"Chiron and I really should double-check the lanterns and make sure the forest is not too suspiciously overgrown." She protests.

"You know how I feel about complaining." I remind her playfully.

Esse finally turns around to look at me, her face still creased with obvious signs of doubt. Through the lines of worry, my little fairy flashes me her best doe-eyed pout. For once, I stand my ground.

"If you are truly concerned for the prosperity of the lanterns and the forests' safety, simply give Chiron and Sam a to-do list. They are very capable you know." I take two thoughtful steps closer to Esse. "Having you present to greet Carlos and his guests would mean a lot. Do not forget, Sela will be expecting you as well." I throw in the last bit knowing that Esse will not be able to resist.

"Alright. If this means so much to you, then I will come quietly." She grins. "Meeting Sela will be nice too."

Esse tries to shrug the matter off as though she is not excited at the prospect of finally meeting my baby sister. Despite Esse's best efforts, I can read her like a book. Her aura tells me that excitement is coursing through her tiny frame like a river through a canyon.

After a final cautious glance back at her field, Esse clambers less than gracefully from the sea of tall grass. As she emerges from the sea of faded green, Esse smooths the wrinkled front of one of her new cotton blend dresses. Seeing her wearing one of the new dresses, makes me happy. I know how much she has missed wearing the dress that was brought from her forest, especially considering the tattered object is Esse's only remaining possession from her centuries spent there.

Thankfully, this particular dress is strikingly similar to her original. The only noticeable difference between the two is that the new one has floral embellishments resembling daisies throughout the bottom edge and is made of more modern materials. Such subtle touches suit Esse well, though she still prefers the natural fibers to which she is accustomed.

I step forward to help her out of the overgrown field, relieved to see her trying not to fly so much. Flying has become so dangerous for her, even on private property. The risk of Esse depleting her energy or being seen by a nosy human with a camera phone has made flying a thing of the past for my fussy little fairy.

Esse takes my arm and smiles. "Well, someone seems to be feeling helpful today." She teases as we pick our way up the slope of the Glade to where the Gator is parked. Esse has made expressly clear the fact that the Gator, and all other motorized vehicles, are not to set tire nor headlight into the glade until after the festivities have concluded.

"I resent that remark. Kiro and I are always helpful." I reply in mock anger.

Esse responds by promptly sticking her tongue out at me like a spoiled child. Her crystal eyes sparkle with fierce mischief.

"Have I not warned you what happens when you stick your tongue out at me, little fairy?"

"Nope." She answers haughtily, shrugging her delicate shoulders with casual bravado.

"You are lucky we have somewhere to be right now or I would show you what happens." I laugh.

We reach the Gator but rather than let Esse climb on herself, I pick her up by her tiny waist and place her on the grey-green machine myself. I pause as she offers her usual complaints at being manhandled. I listen in amusement as she rants for several long-winded seconds, enjoying the heartfelt moment. Having had my fun, I decide it is time to shut her up before she wears herself out or kills me in a freak windstorm.

I press my lips firmly to hers, silencing her mid-rant. Esse's resistance melts away and she is left temporarily stunned by my abrupt gesture. In a fraction of a second, Esse has recovered, her newfound ferocity returning with interest. She returns the spontaneous gesture despite Chiron and Sam's presence in the valley below.

For all of Esse's power and discipline, she still falls apart at the slightest hint of intimacy. Before she has a chance to blow the tops off the trees that she has worked so hard on, I set her down on the Gator.

Best to put a stop to this now before Esse's lack of modesty becomes the least of our concerns. I may not be as barbaric as most members of my species, but that hardly makes me perfect in the department of self-control, especially when Kiro is in one of his neglected moods.

Am not. Kiro argues in an indignant tone.

Oh, spare me! You are a terrible influence when it comes to proximity with Esse.

Your opinion, not mine.

"Well if that is the worst you can come up with, I should make a point of sticking my tongue out more often." Esse chuckles, disrupting my internal dialogue with Kiro.

"If you think that is my worst, then you have not been paying attention these last few months." I laugh, Esse's bold remark having brought a wicked grin to my face.

"So, you never told me how Sela and Andre came to live in Brazil." Esse points out as I slip behind the wheel of the Gator.

"Ironically, Andre and Sela met in Brazil while he and I were tracking her to bring her back home to Europe."

"Wait. Why was she in Brazil to begin with?" Esse leans in against my back, slumping over to rest after all her hard work.

I hesitate before answering her question. Sela's history is tragically typical of a female lycan. However, in this particular story, I happen to be the source of Sela's misfortune.

"She fled to Brazil because of me." I finally admit with a heavy sigh of regret. "Believe it or not, I used to be far more driven in my quest to gain power. Though my intentions were always noble, intentions do not excuse actions or lack thereof. Long story short, I was not there for Sela when she needed me most and she lost her only friend as a result. The grief she suffered as a result of that loss was too much and my little sister fled to Brazil."

"Why Brazil?" Esse asks, surprisingly calm.

"Sela had always wanted to see South America; Brazil just happened to be her destination of choice. Brazil happened to be the place to be at the time."

"I do not understand. Sela and you are so close, much closer than my brother and me. I cannot imagine the two of you...is that why you were so hard on my brother for leaving me?"

"Yes. Your brother repeated my mistakes with you. I suppose I repeated his mistakes with Sela. Either way, seeing my own mistakes reflected upon me so vividly was more than I could stomach."

"Kal, you know full well that we are defined as much by our mistakes as we are by our virtues. Had you not made those mistakes, you might have chosen to fight rather than empathize with me that night in the forest. Who knows what would have become of either of us then?"

"I appreciate the sentiment my little fairy, but I could never have fought you. If there is one thing I know, it is that life without you would not have been worth living. In fact, from the moment you nearly blasted me to bits, I knew that my life was irrevocably altered. You grew up in isolation, so I am sure no one ever explained to you the way most non-humans function hormonally, but we tend to know who our partner is the moment we meet them. This is especially true of someone as old as I am."

"Is that your overly complicated way of telling me that you have always loved me?" she laughs gleefully against my shoulder.

"Yes, I suppose it is." I smile.

"Sela did forgive you even though she stayed in Brazil, right? I mean, the two of you still speak."

"She did." I nod. "The two of you are pretty similar in that regard. Speaking of siblings, how is Har these days?"

"You are deluded in thinking that I am unaware of you changing the subject." She informs me definitively.

"Just humor me." I plead. "Besides, I am sure Sela will be happy to answer all further questions you may have on this matter and my time with you is limited. Let me have this."

She relents, giving a gentle sigh against the side of my neck. "Har is fine. He is still as worried as always, despite my assurance that we will find a way."

Har has every reason to worry. Hell, the situation in the Amazon has me worried. Chiron says that losing the last Great Fairy Tree means certain death for all faeries.

We arrive at the garage on the far right side of the circular driveway and I stop the all-terrain vehicle to let Esse off so she can get ready for Sela's imminent arrival. The lack of discernable heartbeats or voices tells me that our guests have yet to arrive.

Excellent. I should have just enough time to check in with Gus in the kitchen. Dinner should be in its final stages of preparation by now.

By the time I get the tiny vehicle stashed in the garage, Esse is nowhere to be seen.

If she is anything like Sela, and I know she is, our little fairy is upstairs as we speak getting cleaned up. I will have to stop in after talking to Gus, just to make sure she does not need me.

Because you know so much about females preparing to meet other females. Kiro teases playfully.

Fair point. Still, she needs to know that we are here for her, no matter the situation.

I rush to the manor, eager to accomplish my tasks before our guests arrive.

"Gus!" I call out, having barely cleared the doorway to the manor. "How are we fixed for dinner?" I round the corner into the kitchen, elated to see the gruff, former warrior hard at work with his partner in crime by his side. Gus lives for this type of work, especially when he has Doc working alongside him. The dark-skinned omega appears to be enjoying herself almost as much as Gus, her brow furrowed in concentration as she trays up pan after pan of bread loaves.

Doc smiles up at me proudly. "Don't you worry about a thing." She waves her hand casually as if to dismiss a fretful child. "We have everything under control here, you best go check on that fairy of yours. Poor Esse went straight to your bedroom in quite a hurry." Doc informs me.

"If you both are sure you have this..."

"Go, lad!" Gus insists cheerfully. "Ever'thing is shaping up to be a real hooley."

Doc nods her agreement. "Go on, now." For good measure, she makes a shooing motion with her hands.

"Fine. Message received, Doc." I laugh, turning to make my way up the two flights of stairs to our room. Along the way, I stop to check the guest rooms for Carlos and his pack on the third floor. All beds have been properly made and everything appears tidy. The rooms have been well dusted, and the carpets vacuumed. With my mind eased, I hurry toward the room at the end of the hall, painfully aware, already, that the door is open.

Before reaching our room, I am met with an assortment of frustrated grunts and muttering. The source of the ruckus is easily identified as my increasingly incensed little fairy.

Gods help me, what could have her so riled up?

Run? Now? Kiro suggests, only partially joking.

Not an option but I like where your head is at.

I push the door the rest of the way open, knocking lightly on the door frame as I do so, revealing a scene straight out of a Hitchcock film. All over the floral room, dresses and ribbons lay scattered about. The closet stands open, all of its contents spilling out like the insides of an overstuffed burrito.

"Esse…"

Dangling from Esse's silver curls is her white-handled vintage hairbrush, the latest casualty in whatever war has recently taken place in my bedroom. Esse turns to face me, raising her head from where it rests in her palms, her round cheeks as red as ripe tomatoes. I stare speechless at the disheveled creature before me trying to find the right words for the situation.

"Not a word!" She snaps before I have a chance to find any words at all.

I should have listened to you.

Told you so.

I slowly approach Esse, hoping she does not feel inclined to send me flying straight out the door. Reaching up, I warily untangle the ill-fated object from Esse's locks. She offers the faintest huff of objection but allows me to work my magic.

"You know, *if* you would like some help, I am pretty good with basic hairstyling. Before my mother died, I used to braid and brush her hair for her, and my sister, quite a bit. Most Norse women did not keep their hair long back then as it interfered with their ability to fight, but my mother never seemed hindered by hers. Nonetheless, she kept her hair braided or pulled back always. Above all other styles, my mother favored intricate braids."

Talking about my mother seems to disarm Esse. Her cheeks slowly return to their usual ivory tone, and the corners of her mouth curl into the beginnings of a smile.

"Can you do this?" Esse produces a scrap of paper from a magazine with a picture of a woman on it. The woman's hair, which is clearly not meant to be the focus of the photograph, is pulled back at the sides into two braids that meet at the back of her head. The style is relatively simple but not a common look amongst faeries.

She has come so far, I sometimes forget that she still knows so little about living in the modern, human world.

"Of course I can do that." I lift Esse's chin and kiss the top of her head in a reassuring gesture. "Sit down and let me work my own patented brand of magic." I reach around the side of her waist and pull up the chair that rests in front of her mahogany dresser which boasts a wide ornate mirror with copper leaves in the upper corners. She takes her seat and fluffs her sunflower dress nervously.

"Relax my precious little fairy. Have some faith; I know that you want to look nice for Sela, just do not forget that your hair does not define you. Sela is not focused on such attributes. Besides, you always look beautiful, especially to me. My sister will see that beauty too."

"I know how *you* feel, you are not exactly subtle." She grins. "I just want to make a good first impression and be my best self, that is all."

"Do you want to tell me what is bothering you?" I probe as I pull the curls from the right side of her hair back and carefully weave them into a single, intricate braid along the center of the right side of Esse's head.

84

"I am not sure how to explain." She responds honestly.

"This is me here." I smile earnestly. "Just talk and I am sure I will figure it out."

"Well, I have this feeling that everything is going to change. I cannot explain how or why, I just feel as though my days of being able to walk free like you and Doc and Gus and Red...I feel like those days are numbered even though they just began. I know that is a foolish thing to say without any evidence, but I just want to make the most of every moment anyway."

I do not like this. Kiro chimes in, stirring from his brief rest deep in the back of our shared mind.

She speaks the truth, even if she has not fully accepted it as such yet. Eventually, she will have wings, though who knows when that will be. However, the feelings she is having are worrisome.

The last time Esse had a strange feeling about the future was just before she cut her knee swimming with Kiro. That turned out to be a harbinger of death like none other. Shortly after that injury, she lost her home to the Order.

As I contemplate the prophetic nature of Esse's emotions, I continue to pull her hair carefully into a braid. I slowly progress from the right side to the left until the two braids meet at the back of Esse's head.

I reach forward and open a drawer on my side of the dresser. My rummaging in the tiny drawer draws Esse's attention.

"What are you looking for in there?" she asks quietly.

"Something that I think will make you happy, and help you make the most of every moment as you wanted."

"Does this something have a name?" she laughs. "What item, small enough to fit in that drawer, could possibly help me now?"

Happy to see a bit of cheer returning to her unusually gloomy face, I smile at my little fairy. "You will see when I find what I am looking for."

After a few more seconds of rummaging, I manage to locate the object: a palm-sized, blue and green jade butterfly pin dating back to the fifteenth century. The delicate artifact is a gift from my days spent in Asia.

Esse's eyes light up, sparkling with intrigue as she sets her gaze upon the tiny object, which is every bit as delicate in appearance as Esse herself. For such a simple pin, the object's beauty is undeniable.

"Where did you get such a thing?" she asks breathlessly, her eyes fixed to the pin in wonder. "The butterfly is so beautiful! Much more naturally beautiful than anything in those shops we visited in town."

"I figured you would appreciate the design. Remember our discussion of my travels to China?"

She nods excitedly, her eyes still fixed to the object like a dog staring at a bowl of food.

"Well, China is where this little object came from. I have always had this thing about not keeping my nose out of it when a female is in danger."

"You do not say..." Esse cuts me off narrowing her eyes suspiciously, a wicked grin creeping across her reflection in the mirror.

"Down little attack fairy. Let us not forget, I am still fixing your hair at the moment. The fate of your silver curls is literally in my hands." I remind her jokingly, though I know her wrath, when genuine, is no joke.

"Yes, yes. Just finish your story and then I will decide if the situation warrants me sending you flying out of our window at the expense of my hair."

That is our girl. Kiro boasts. Kiro's growing pride in Esse's newfound ferocity should concern me or at least warrant discussion, but I am already lost in my nostalgic tale.

"While traveling through one of China's provinces, in what is now central China, I met a young lycan by the name of Jade.

Coincidentally, that is what the pin is made of. She did not say much about her history, but the impression I got from our initial encounter was that she was in deep."

"What do you mean?" Esse arches an eyebrow at me in the mirror as I begin the final touches on her hair.

"Well, I was on my way to the coast in search of a magus that was rumored to be in possession of an artifact Don required. Along the way, this strange lycanthrope female decided to try and rob me using a broken wagon as bait. As if such a pedestrian tactic would ever work on me."

"Broken wagon?"

"Yes. Wagons were the primary form of travel at that time. Automobiles have only been around for about a century and a half and for most of that time, only the wealthy had the privilege of owning one."

"So wagons were operated without engines?" Esse deduces.

"Correct. They were typically wooden framed and pulled by large beasts such as horses, oxen, or mules. Jade pretended hers was broken so that I would stop to help her. Then, had her plan succeeded, she would have jumped me, knocked me unconscious, and stolen my possessions. However, her scheme failed as I saw right through her little rouse."

"How did you see through it?" Esse chirps excitedly, her interest in the story having peaked.

"Well, firstly, the trick is an obvious one. Secondly, she did not smell like horse or ox."

"That is all? The wagon was a trick because Jade did not smell like a horse?"

"If there had been beasts pulling her cart recently, she and the cart would have smelled of horse or ox. Instead, both smelled clean."

"Oh. Then how did she expect to trick anyone? She does not seem terribly smart." Esse declares triumphantly.

"She was not expecting a non-human target. Humans do not possess the same sense of smell that I do." I laugh, feeling a mix of pride and amusement at Esse's mildly territorial reaction.

"So why was she trapping strangers and why on earth would you want to help someone who tried to rob you?"

"The answer to that question lies in her motives. You see, Jade was stealing because she was desperate and scared. Her scrawny form, shifting gaze, and distinct nervousness in the presence of men was a dead giveaway."

A thoughtful silence ensues. Esse seems to understand what I am trying not to say. Such signs are clear indicators of the hell that awaits all female lycans.

"Anyway." I continue, clearing my throat as if to dispel the solemn mood that now hangs in the air like the curtain of a grand opera stage. "As luck would have it, Jade was aiming to charter a vessel from the coast, so she tagged along with me."

"And she gave you the pin."

"Yes," I confirm. "She gave me the pin; it was all she had left after chartering her boat."

"What happened to her?" Esse asks as I finish pinning her hair with the jade butterfly.

"I cannot say as I have not seen her since that day. Something tells me she is out there in the world somewhere, biding her time until the day when lycans like her can be free."

"I think you are right. All the more reason for you to succeed in your mission." Esse points out.

"That is the plan, and with your help, we might just succeed. In any case, I believe we are done here. Just in time by the looks of it."

"They are here!" Esse turns around excitedly in her chair, nearly knocking it over in the process.

"They should be pulling up any second now," I inform her. "The sound of three rental cars is very distinct to my ears."

"By the Goddess, I love lycanthrope hearing!" she grins up at me and leaps excitedly from her chair. She pauses for a moment to take one final look in the mirror. "This is a beautiful little pin."

I step forward, delighted to see her in such high spirits, and lightly kiss the top of her head. "The butterfly pin reminds me of you. Are you ready to finally meet her?"

"Are you kidding? I thought this day would never come!" She takes off down the stairs, moving at the speed of the wind.

"Slow down Esse, before you fall down those stairs!" I call after her.

"You know full well that faeries cannot fall down the stairs!" she calls back mischievously. Her enthusiasm having reached infectious levels.

With a shake of my head and one final, longing glance back at the safety of our room, I follow Esse downstairs. As I pass the kitchen, I call out to Gus and Doc.

"The guests of honor are pulling up now, you two! Plan for dinner on the table in half an hour or less."

"Aye, we guessed as much lad. The lass came barreling down the stairs like a train, she did." Gus laughs from the kitchen, bringing a smile to my face.

Doc pokes her head out to give me the details on the situation behind the scenes. "Coffee is ready to roll and Gus took the liberty of stocking the beer fridge and wine cooler in the den for our guests." She smiles warmly.

"I knew I could count on the two of you."

I catch up to Esse who has frozen in the entryway. Her aura has shifted from one of unbridled excitement to a sphere of writhing nerves and frayed tension.

"Just breathe. I assure you, none of them bite." I whisper lightly into her ear as I brush smoothly past her to let in the guests rapidly approaching the manor door. I reach slowly for the door handle and pull open the broad doors. In doing so, I find myself nearly run over by my ill-mannered hurricane of a sister.

"Brother!" Sela roars with a volume that could wake the dead. A tiny, yet perfectly placed, burst of wind from Esse keeps me upright despite the chokingly strong hug laid upon me by my beloved sister.

"Good to see you too little sister," I growl in slight irritation, patting her on the shoulder happily.

"Oh don't be cross big brother." Sela puffs out her bottom lip in an eerily familiar mocking pout.

She and Esse are far too similar for my liking. I observe.

"Of course it is good to see you Sela, but there are far better ways to say hello than running over your only brother."

"When have you ever known her to do anything the easy way?" A bass deep, familiar voice rises from behind Sela.

"Andre! It is great to see you again, old friend." I call out to the hulking figure now looming over my sister's shoulder. The goliath, dark-skinned lycanthrope has not changed a bit since I last saw him.

"Make room Sela. Everyone is quite tired and famished. We all know how long flights can make even the most tempered lycans grumpy. Besides princess, you have four whole days to catch up with your brother." Andre herds Sela out of the path of the rest of their restless pack.

The gentle giant's smile is so genuine, though his words, as always, are as serious as a judge's verdict. When it comes to pack matters, Andre is a very serious man. Otherwise, the intimidating mountain of a man is little more than an overgrown child. Sela tenses slightly but nods, stepping out of the way.

"Sela, this is Esse. How about you let her show you to the room where Andre and you will be staying."

"So," Sela turns to Esse with a mile-wide grin, "you are the famous Ellesse, sister to the king of the faeries. I am glad to finally meet you."

The two of them strike up an animated conversation as Sela picks up her bag from the spot where she carelessly abandoned it moments ago. With all the haste and energy of two young children, the girls make their way down the hall toward the stairs.

With Esse at ease and Sela occupied, I turn my attention to where I am needed most. Stepping back, I allow Andre to brush past me to the right so that the irritable, jet-lagged bunch of lycans waiting outside can enter the manor. A tall, thin, olive-skinned lycan steps through the doorway first. He is followed by two more lycans of similar build and skin tone.

"You remember Carlos and his brothers, Julio and Ray, from your last trip to Brazil." Andre addresses me while keeping his gaze focused squarely on Carlos and his brothers.

I cast a worried look in Andre's direction. The last time I saw the De Santos brothers, there were more of them.

"The Order took Juan from us. Antonio was lost to Feng's initial resistance." Carlos answers my unspoken question, sensing my concern.

"You have my sincerest apologies, Carlos. I can assure you; Feng's little rebellion has been dealt with."

"If only the mongrel himself were dealt with. But that is a story to end another day. My brothers' sharp ears tell me that you have coffee."

"Doc has it ready and waiting in the dining room. There is also beer and wine in the den, you all are welcome to help yourselves for the entirety of your stay."

"Always the generous host." Carlos cracks a brief smile before continuing down the hall.

"Find Esse upstairs, she will show you and your brothers to your rooms," I inform the young prime alpha.

"Ah, no need to trouble the girls. I remember where they are." Andre insists.

Carlos nods and makes his way toward the stairs, followed by his brothers. The string of lycans lined up outside follow their alpha, eager to drop their bags and head to dinner. As planned, there are roughly fifteen lycans in total, just short of three-quarters of Carlos' pack.

While Andre shows them the way, I make a quick sweep of the dining room and den to make sure everything is as it should be. Within moments, Andre has returned downstairs, alone.

"I take it you folks left the others to hold down the fort." I turn and find that Andre's face, on close inspection, is worn with a weariness I have never seen in my jovial friend.

"The situation with the humans has worsened, my friend. This *is* our pack."

The grave reality of his words takes several moments to sink in. Carlos may be hot-headed, but he is also as careful as they come. If the Order found his pack, then it is only a matter of time before they come for my family as well.

Esse. Kiro's mind steadily fills with anguished thoughts of Esse dying in all manner of horrifying scenarios. Such thoughts echo my deep-seated fears.

I know. She is as good as dead once her wings come in.

"How did this happen?" I question, carefully suppressing the dread rising inside me. The last thing I need is for Andre to worry about my state of mind.

"We are not entirely sure. What we do know is that the Order is packing more firepower than they ever have before. As far as I could tell from my brief interactions with them, they are using magic now…*dark* magic. I know that sounds insane, which is probably why Carlos dismissed it, but I swear I have seen the signs. Juan's body had *all* of the signs. The blood surrounding his wounds was blackened and foul, his body began to rot immediately, and the site where we found him was tainted with the stench of sulfur."

"I believe you, Andre. Back in Esse's forest, she and I witnessed things we could not explain. Ellesse says one of the Order members was controlling a wraith using a strange staff."

"Only a demon can command such a beast," Andre growls in horror.

"I forget that you are well versed in the old ways of magic."

"Believe me, there are days when I wish I could forget the old ways. If the human race finds a way to weaponize demonic magic, then we are all dead...including the humans. Dark magic does not follow the laws of nature that bind and dictate our world; if used without proper cause and restraint, such magic will eventually tear apart our world."

"Is it true, what the legends say, that their magic is *actual* magic?" I ask my old friend, finding myself oddly curious.

"That would depend upon your definition of magic. Though I have never seen the other side with my own eyes, the stories say that, on the hell plane, magic is no different than the natural forces that govern our world. Take, for instance, force, a well-defined concept here on Earth. The laws that govern force as we know it do not exist on the hell plane. Therefore, the way creatures interact with one another, and their environment, there may seem magical to us by comparison. To the inhabitants of the hell plane, the demon race, our world is relatively primitive. The demons understand the laws that govern their world because their creator ingrained such information into their minds. We can only hope to have such an understanding of our world one day."

"That day will come long after you and I are gone, old friend." I laugh, grateful for the lesson on dark magic.

I step forward and place a hand on Andre's shoulder. "You have not changed. Your knowledge of the many worlds that comprise our universe is as profound as always."

Andre flashes me a thankful smile before shaking his head in a gesture of physical and mental exhaustion.

"Why does it feel like all we have ever done is fight? Is it so difficult for the creatures of this world to just be happy? Is there not room for us all in this world?" Andre laments.

"If memory serves, you were close to Juan. I can only imagine how difficult his death must have been for you and Carlos."

"Juan was unrecognizable when we found him. His left leg was gone along with his right arm. His left arm was shattered, and his abdomen was ripped open as was his chest. The look of agony on his face...no one deserves to go like that." Andre's voice is rife with anguish.

I cannot help picturing what Esse would have looked like had I not gotten to her in time the day her forest burned.

"You have my word that I will fix this mess of a broken world. I will bring peace and give our people back the freedom we once knew when humans had not the power to dishonor this world the way they do. But first things first, comes fixing our people. How can we ever expect the humans to do right by us if we cannot do right by ourselves?" I declare with a confidence I thought I lacked.

Andre nods his appreciation then lifts his head toward the staircase just beyond the door to the dining room. I turn to see Carlos approaching us.

"Just could not wait for that coffee I see." For once, I am glad to entertain. The grim nature of my conversation with Andre was beginning to rattle me.

"You would be itching for caffeine as well after thirteen hours on a plane," Carlos grumbles in a mostly humorous tone.

"At least you did not have to babysit a fairy." I retort in wry humor.

"Fair enough!" Carlos smiles, finally dropping the veil of professionalism behind which he hides as an alpha of a relatively newly formed pack. Carlos is accustomed to hiding behind his professional bravado in front of the other alphas in his territory.

The young alpha makes his way to the promised coffee with eager strides. I decide that it is best to wait before approaching the subject of his brothers until after the volatile leader has had his first cup of coffee.

While waiting, Ray and Julio appear, as silently as cats in the snow, from the hallway. Like their brother, the two hurry to pour themselves some coffee. I watch, somewhat enviously, as the three brothers make themselves comfortable and Andre departs to find Sela before dinner. Though the loss of a sibling could not have been easy, at least Carlos and the other De Santos siblings had one another. With Sela having been in Brazil for decades now, I have found myself feeling lonely for the first time in many centuries.

We have Esse now. Kiro offers sympathetically, knowing the familiar sense of loneliness all too well.

I smile in my head, grateful for Kiro's genuine compassion. Though he can be a stubborn and unpredictable wolf, Kiro is also more reliable than most wolves I have encountered.

"Andre told me about Juan, and Antonio too." I decide to bring up Carlos' departed brothers before anyone else can arrive for dinner. "I hope all of you know that I have not forgotten about the threat the humans pose and all that they have done. I will find us a solution, no matter what it takes. You have my word on that."

"We are aware that you of all of us have the most to lose here. She is very kind and energetic by the way. I can see how you favor her." To my surprise, it is Ray who speaks first.

"Careful. Ellesse may seem cute and tiny but she is as lethal as a jaguar, even to primes."

The brothers laugh, though Carlos at least seems to understand that I am only half-joking. Before anything more can be said, the echo of several lycan voices, accompanied by the thundering of a dozen sets of boots on stairs, tells me it is time to get dinner on the table.

"Gus!" I call out to the busy lycan in case he is too absorbed in his work to hear the hoard outside in the hallway.

"Aye hear them." He calls back in a thick accent, indicating that he is fully immersed in the task before him.

The hoard of visibly refreshed albeit famished Brazilian lycans pile into the dining room like a thunderous herd of elk. Doc appears, just in time, carrying the first trays of food. Each of the two trays she carries is stacked perilously with platters and dishes each boasting an assortment of meat, vegetables, bread, or cheese.

As she places the last of the platters on the table, Gus appears behind her beaming with pride as he brings in his famous four meat chili in a pot that could hold a small child.

"Doc, hun, could ya grab the bowls from the kitchen for me?"

"Of course, love. Looks like we will need more bread anyway." Doc disappears back into the mystic fog of steam and cooking smoke that is our kitchen. Before she has the chance to return, with Gus still carefully guarding his precious chili, the Brazilians descend upon the table like a pack of ravenous hyenas.

"You see! We will be lucky to get scraps now. While you ladies were catching up, they went a started without us in true wolf form." Andre growls in playful complaint, shaking his head at Esse and Sela as the trio makes their way into the dining room.

"Relax Andre. I am sure my brother will see to it that you do not go unfed, not that we need him to secure food for us." Sela soothes in her special blend of sarcasm and sincerity.

With a final sly glance in Andre's direction, my somewhat feral sister dives into the fray.

"That's my little warrior princess!" Andre praises before diving in alongside Sela, never one to be left out when food is involved.

With the addition of Andre and Sela, the scene before me makes for the perfect snapshot of lycanthrope festivity. Such scenes are increasingly rare of late given the growing threats from lycans and humans alike. Still, seeing the primary Brazilian pack gathered under one roof without worry gives me cause for hope.

Red appears, having cleaned himself up after another long day of repairs and car maintenance.

"Brought the twins." He announces simply.

"Looks like we made it just in time!" Annie declares, her stomach audibly growling at the sight of the rapidly diminishing feast. She hastily throws off her jacket and rushes to find a spot at the table amidst the chaos. Dex simply shakes his head at his feral sister, flashing me a look of comradery in acknowledgment of our shared plight as brothers, before casually joining his boisterous sister.

"Sorry, we are late. We got caught up in traffic on the way over and of course, work was hell. Could not get out of there to save my life. The suits just cannot stand me taking off for any length of time." Dex laughs as he makes his way to the table.

"No worries Dex. Enjoy your hard-earned dinner...if you can pry any away from them that is." I laugh, finding myself in an unusually joyous mood.

Dex pauses before reaching the throng of ravenous lycans. "This is nice. Is it just me, or does something about this just seem...right?"

"I suppose this does feel right. If only I could find a way to make this our reality." I respond longingly.

"No need to worry about that right now, this is a party after all! Besides, you will get us there, and we will be right here beside you the whole way. We all believe in you, Kal." Dex informs me.

Before I can question his words, Esse steps up beside me and places her hand on my upper arm.

"You should listen to him. After all, you are always saying there is no better strategist than Dex. That big brain of his knows what it is talking about."

Esse stares up at me from my right shoulder with the same sparkle in her storm-cloud eyes that I saw the night I met her.

Perhaps she is right. I suppose the future I have envisioned for so long could be more than a dream after all.

"Are you not going to eat?" Esse asks me, leaning into my shoulder lazily.

"I will eat later," I assure her.

Dex finds his place at the table while Esse and I watch on in content silence. The two of us stand shoulder to shoulder in the entrance of the dining room as the table slowly empties of food. As the food disappears, the now satisfied lycans slowly rise and disperse into smaller clusters throughout the ground floor of the manor. As the lycans exit the dining room, two or three at a time, a puzzled look forms on Esse's face.

"Why are there no women among them? I know you said the rate of female births is low among lycans, but our pack is small, and we have two females. How can a pack as large as theirs have only Sela? She said this is the entire pack...I just do not understand."

I should have guessed she would ask a question like this sooner than later.

She is clever. Kiro affirms.

How do I explain to her the brutality of a pack that she views as our friend and ally?

As if to save me, an unexpected voice breaks into our hushed conversation.

"I could not help overhearing," Carlos interjects. "What do you know of my pack's history?" The young alpha inquires, addressing me more so than Esse.

"Not much. I heard talk of great brutality under your father's reign. I recall your uncle being rather brutal as well. Women were disposed of fairly regularly for failing to contribute to the male bloodlines. In rare cases, I have heard of females being taken from surrounding territories and smuggled into your uncle's territory. Sometime in the last century, there was a turnover which resulted in you taking control of the pack and uniting all of the smaller packs in the area under one sphere of influence."

"All of that is true, though your version of events barely scratches the surface." Carlos nods in approval rising from his chair.

"I do not normally tell this story, but for you, I shall make an exception." Carlos pulls out a chair for Esse across the table from where he and his brothers have been sitting.

Esse throws a nervous glance in my direction before turning to take the seat offered to her.

"Why do I get the feeling this is not going to be a pleasant story?" Esse shifts nervously in the chair as Carlos returns to his seat.

I step forward to stand protectively behind her, hoping to give her some assurance of security despite the tragic nature of what she is about to hear. I place a soothing hand on Esse's shoulder and smile down at her.

You are safe with me. This is just a story; it cannot hurt you. I assure her telepathically. Though she cannot hear or read my thoughts, thanks to her strange connection to Kiro, Esse can receive basic emotions and images through my mind.

"Happy or not, this is my story and, coincidentally, the reason why I take the risk of backing Greyback," Carlos states, drawing a strange tension from Esse at the mention of the word *Greyback*.

"You see," Carlos continues, "my father was a harsh man, but he was not exactly the monster everyone thought him to be. Though time hardened him in many ways, he never lost his love for certain aspects of life, including art, music, and beauty. My father had the distinct misfortune of loving my mother and his sons very much. He took every precaution not to let the world see how he felt, knowing that his weakness would certainly condemn us all to a painful death. Our family, including my uncle, we sons, and my grandfather, did eventually take notice over time as my father slowly lowered his guard."

"There were originally seven of us boys. Her fertility kept our mother in our grandfather's good graces despite the threat she posed to my father's reputation and loyalty." Ray adds to his brother's explanation.

"However, our uncle was not so kind. Our uncle was known for being a bitter and sadistic man. The world believes wholeheartedly that our father killed our mother." Carlos continues.

"But he would never do that. Not if he loved her the way you said he did. The way Kal speaks has made it clear to me that lycanthropes who come to accept their feelings for one another are not able to break free of those feelings so easily." Esse interjects.

"Perhaps. Perhaps not. We may never know the truth of my father's feelings. What we do know is that one night, our uncle went on a rampage and made it his prerogative to vent that rage on our youngest brother, Romeo. This was when our mother was still alive. She refused to stand for our uncle's tirade. Though she never would have said so, Romeo was always her favorite. She intervened and paid with her life. Romeo died of his injuries. My father flew into a rage of his own, killing our uncle and his only son, ending our uncle's line. When our grandfather confronted our father a bloody fight ensued. And so, our father killed his father."

"You are right. This is not a happy story." Esse pauses, looking sick for a moment, then continues. "You said there were seven of you?"

"Clever girl." Ray grins earning the tiniest growl of warning from Kiro.

Esse reaches up to place one small hand over my own to soothe me and my angry wolf as Carlos concludes his tragic tale.

"Flash forward about fifty years or so and our dear baby brother, Esteban, decides he is sick of playing the role of baby brother. The runt grew tired of taking dad's orders and bearing the brunt of our father's newfound bitterness. Losing a brother, father, wife, and son would leave any man hollow after all. Esteban cut off our father's head while he slept and attempted to have each of us killed as well."

"The fact that we three still sit here should tell you how that went for him," Ray adds.

"The other two brothers?" Esse questions.

"Unrelated incidents," Carlos answers, keeping the topic of the Order to himself for the time being.

Esse remains pensive for a moment before inquiring further. "This level of violence, it seems so common among lycanthropes."

This time it is my turn to answer Esse's implied question. "This is one of the more pleasant stories I have heard, as tragic as it may seem."

"Kal is right. His story, more than anyone else's, is rife with tragedy." Carlos adds.

"We should rest," Julio speaks up, breaking his long silence.

"Of course." The brothers agree.

"We enjoyed seeing all of you tonight. If you need anything let us know." I inform them.

The brothers depart, leaving Esse and me alone in the dining room, with Doc and Gus still finishing up the cleaning in the kitchen. The voices of the twins and several Brazilian lycanthropes drift in from the den. After a few moments of silence, Esse finally asks the question that has been looming in her mind since our ill-fated encounter with Feng.

"What did Feng mean when he spoke of your reputation and why is Carlos insinuating that your story is more tragic than his? I get the feeling that they are not just referring to the death of your father." She deduces cleverly.

"You remember what happened to my mother and father I am sure. I thought I could live with all I had lost, that I could move on. For a time, I did move on. Then I passed back through Norway, the area where my pack originally lived in what became my territory. As fate would have it, my dad's old pack had merged with an Irish bloodline that contained the prime gene as well, which allowed them to regain their former strength of numbers. Let us just say, my past came back to haunt me in a bad way when I ran into some of my father's old pack, who did not recognize me after all the centuries that had passed. Unfortunately for them, I will never forget their faces. I lost control in a bad way. The exact events of that night are a blur, but when my head finally cleared, not one of the Irish/Norse pack remained."

"You killed them all," Esse murmurs questioningly.

Her words hurt me more than seeing the faces of the men who mercilessly robbed Sela and me of our parents ever could have.

She did not mean it. Kiro offers.

Why should she not be disappointed in us? That day was not our best.

Our worst day, but she still loves us.

Kiro makes an excellent point. Though Esse's aura conveys a deep concern for the gravity of my actions, there is no animosity in what she feels. If anything, I would classify her feelings as those of profound sympathy or even remorse, as though my actions were somehow her fault.

Despite Esse's feelings, I find myself drifting into a fog of self-hatred. Even after the passage of nearly a century, I can still hear the sounds of each lycan dying amid a hellish blur of crimson fury.

It was not just you. Kiro whimpers from a dark corner deep inside the fortress of my mind.

That is not fair to you. Kiro, you did nothing wrong. Balancing our mental state is a team effort and I failed you.

You did not force me...I missed them too. Kiro admits, vivid images of our parents' faces filling his mind. Much to my surprise, he even recalls the auburn wolf of my mother and the silver-gray wolf of my father with near perfection. I had almost forgotten what their wolves looked like.

A gentle touch against the side of my face disrupts our internal pity party. Esse's delicate fingers slowly trace the jagged line of the scar that runs down the side of my neck.

"I get it now. Greyback is not a title, it is your family name."

"For someone whose species does not use family names, you catch on to them fairly quick. The Greyback line is dead now; it died with my father."

"You may have done some awful things in the past, but you have also done immeasurable good with the time you have been given since. Please do not…beat yourself up? Did I say that correctly?" Esse smiles warmly, her eyes soft and full of empathetic kindness.

"You said it perfectly, sweetie." Doc's voice draws my attention to the doorway. "She is right by the way. You will always be Kal O'Connell to us. Though you could have been just a bit more inspired with the name choice." Doc points out.

"I like it." Esse chirps.

What is with the women in my life insulting me as they reassure me? Is this some new trend?

Every day for me. Kiro teases.

"On that note, my little fairy, it is time for bed. We have a big day tomorrow. Doc you and Gus get some rest too, we made you guys a room upstairs. Gus will know which one is for you." I turn my attention to a now pouting little fairy. "Still not afraid to share a bed with a confirmed killer?"

"Do not say such things! You know me better than that. There is no place I would rather sleep."

Six

As the evening sun begins to set, its brilliant beams of fading light setting the horizon ablaze with vibrant pink, red, and orange waves against cloudy ripples, the Brazilians dive eagerly into the Fall Moon Feast celebration.

"Ya see lass, Fall Moon Feast celebrations, also known as the Winter's Nights celebration, twas once a night for a celebration of the final harvest for the year before winter set in," Gus explains to a wide-eyed Ellesse dressed in one of her green silk sundresses.

Esse sits across from Gus on one of the stone benches, her feet dangling slightly. Beside her sits Chiron, happy to have his wings out for once, though he keeps them folded subtly behind him. As the Brazilians have slowly arrived in the valley glade, each has stared in fascination at Chiron's brilliant, gem-like wings. Most lycans have never seen a set of fairy wings in their lives, nor will they ever so long as faeries remain hidden away.

"But now we just use the festival as an excuse to celebrate and eat great food and drink even better ale," Dex adds to Gus's informative tale, forever polluting the mind of my little fairy.

"Lots of that last bit." Annie piles on.

"And this is the first year that all of you are hosting Carlos and his family?" Esse asks, taking a bite from the apple she has been twirling absent-mindedly in her right hand.

"That is correct, my little fairy. You helped inspire that long-awaited change. Ale and food aside, we should not forget our heritage or the importance of the feast. Back before the age of technology, when one bad harvest could spell death even for lycans, this feast was a way to appeal to the minor gods of harvest. Some call these gods Vanir." I explain.

"All the more reason to be grateful we made this year's festival extra special!" She boasts.

Her whimsical outburst and wide-eyed wonder earn her a resounding cheer and rumble of laughter from those already gathered in the glade.

"You certainly did outdo yourselves with that fairy magic of yours."

"Sela!" Esse leaps up excitedly from her place on the cold stone bench to greet my sister as she and Andre approach.

"Do you like what we did with the place?" Esse asks, her hands clasped tightly in front of her in anticipation.

"How could anyone with eyes not love this? I have not seen Ireland looking so beautiful and at peace, since I was young, and humans still used horses to move about! This place was little more than a field the last time I saw it. Now this glade is so full of life! Even the lake is brimming with happy fish. We can scarcely call it a glade anymore for all the plant life you have added here. Look, Andre, actual trees and flowers are growing here now."

Sela takes in the glade with the same look of wonder I was left with when Esse showed me the special trees in her Canadian forest where the butterflies would migrate each year. The cloud of butterflies would coat the trees in a living carpet of vibrant color that was truly a sight to behold, at least according to Esse.

What a shame that we never had the privilege of seeing the butterflies with our own eyes. The trees were something in their own right though.

Even Kiro is struck with a pang of genuine sadness at the realization that those butterflies no longer have that special place to go back to. To cheer us both up, I see fit to add to Sela's praise of my little fairy's handy work.

"She even grew the trees that produced the apples for the targets, and she grew the vines for the pumpkins. Chiron was equally amazing with all his efforts growing up the foliage around the lake so that we could let the wolves run without risking a drone sighting."

105

"He was going to *buy* pumpkins. With two perfectly adept faeries right here, one does not simply buy pumpkins." Esse rolls with playful laughter.

"Yes, clearly I was not thinking straight." I wave my hand dramatically in mock exasperation earning a pouting frown from my precious fairy and a knowing grin from Sela.

"Keep pushing her and you will wind up plant food." Sela laughs, not realizing how right she is. Esse is no pushover, after all.

"He is too useful to feed to the plants." Esse grins mischievously.

Do not start. I warn the notoriously amorous Kiro, knowing that he is thinking exactly as I am.

I did not start it. She started it.

Well, I am ending it. We have guests to tend to.

Later. Kiro decides.

My body, my timeline horny wolf. Now go do whatever you do for a bit.

With a huff of mock indignation, Kiro settles himself.

Sela lets out a roaring laugh, drawing the attention of all gathered at the table.

"I have never seen anyone disarm and incapacitate my brother so easily." Sela pants through her laughter.

"Now, now princess. Take it easy on your brother. I feel his pain, you know." Andre steps forward, coming to my defense, and places a hand on Sela's hunched shoulders.

She straightens immediately to meet his inviting gaze. A knowing smile forms on both their faces. Finding a partner that can literally share your thoughts is a once-in-a-lifetime experience that only a dozen species on this earth will ever know. Some lycans will go their entire lives without ever knowing the joy of being so close to another creature. That is the cross borne by creatures like us who must spend our lives hiding who and what we are from the world, forever divided from that world and one another.

"Lads and lasses, one and all, dinner is served!" Gus bellows from the glade's center to a chorus of excited roars and thunderous cheers.

Everyone scrambles to fill their mugs with ale from the aged oak kegs Gus brought out after lunch, shoving and fighting spiritedly amongst themselves to get a good seat at the stone tables. The scent of ale and meat fills the air as plates are filled to the brim and mugs collide, ale sloshing over the rims and into the earth below.

"Last to the table again," Andre growls in childlike frustration. "Good thing I saved a chicken for myself while Gus was in the kitchen this afternoon."

Sela throws up her hands playfully as she slowly backs away toward the rowdy brood and enticing selection of meats, vegetables, and cheeses. Andre's eyes light up with dark excitement, as though some unspoken game has just been initiated with Sela and Andre as the solitary participants.

"Princess..." Andre's voice is little more than a low growl, though his eyes still twinkle with excitement.

Sela's only response to Andre's endearing nickname for her is to grin mischievously back at him, then dive for a particular seat on the stone table closest to Gus.

"That is *my* chicken you little she-demon!" Andre roars, wasting no time in diving after his agile partner.

"Then come and get it, slowpoke!" Sela laughs triumphantly, knowing she has the speed advantage. She does not look back at the now visibly excited, mocha-skinned, warrior.

Esse turns back to me with a puzzled look on her face. "Am I supposed to understand what that was about?"

"Everyone has their own unique means of communicating with their partner. That was their way." I explain.

"Fighting over meat?" She raises an eyebrow at me questioningly.

"Yes, they fight over meat." I reiterate though I am still a bit confused.

"So what is our thing?" Esse asks half-jokingly.

"When our lives calm down enough for us to find it, I will let you know exactly what our thing is." I tease, burying my face in the top of her silky hair.

I have to admit, I did not expect to feel this relaxed today. I confide in Kiro.

Enjoy it. He responds happily.

You should enjoy it as well. Don assures me his cameras and security sensors are sound. Take the night off!

Later. Kiro insists.

Party pooper. I tease, attempting to relax my noticeably tense wolf.

"You two must be having quite the conversation." Esse interrupts, her head tilted up toward mine, with her round eyes fixed on my face in mild amusement.

"Kiro is just being extra vigilant," I inform her. "Nothing to worry about."

Esse eyes us suspiciously for a moment but shrugs off any concern she may have. Today is as joyful a day for her as it is for me, after all.

"Well, if the two of you are fine, do you mind if I go find Sela after she eats? There is still so much I want to ask her about."

"That sounds like a wonderful idea, not that you need to ask my permission. Have fun, just go easy on my sister." I plead.

She wiggles her way into my arms for a hug before darting off excitedly to catch up to Sela, who appears to be in deep, over at the table. Before I have time to miss her, Gus's thunderous voice drifts over from the fighting ring.

"How about we get these festivities underway now that ever'one has been fed, eh?"

"That sounds like a grand idea Gus! What say you, Carlos?" I call out.

A chorus of excited cheers rises from the participants gathered in the valley of the glade.

"It would seem my pack has spoken," Carlos responds with a wicked grin.

With their alpha's approval secured, the Brazilian pack pours into the dugout seats of the ring while Andre, who must have devoured his chicken in record time, sets up pairings for each round. The air in the valley comes alive with excitement.

Well officer killjoy, ready to grab a drink and place some friendly bets?

Am not a killjoy. I am Kiro.

I know your name!

I stifle a laugh at Kiro's childlike stubbornness. Despite his resistance, I can sense the excitement in my wolf.

We make our way to the stacked barrels that Gus set up between Chiron's cabin and the stone tables for the feast.

This is why. Kiro remarks as we stumble upon a rare scene of mischief: a heavily intoxicated Dex.

"Ah come on Doc. There is nothing wrong with that there ale. I have had so much of it...wouldn't I be dead if it were bad?" Dex slurs, stumbling slightly to his right.

"I am sorry, do you have a doctorate in medicine or chemistry that I do not know about?" Doc retorts dryly. "How would you know anyway? You are visibly drunk off your ass! You could be dying right now, and you would not even know it Dex. How much ale is even required for a lycan to achieve such a level of intoxication?"

"Easy. Keep your voices down, please. What exactly is the problem?" I interject before the pair can draw unwelcome attention and sully the mood of the evening.

Kiro shifts restlessly but keeps his concerns to himself for once.

"Finally, someone with some sense." Doc throws up her hands in a gesture of frustration, whirling around to face me. She brandishes a ladle in my direction.

"Using the ladle already?" I grin cleverly. "Is the tap not pouring fast enough for you?"

"The tap is busted." She growls, unamused. "That is beside the point. Kal, I tasted this ale myself last night and I swear something is off with it today."

"Relax Doc; you can be a perfectionist. Are you sure the weather did not get to it?"

"I have three PhDs and it is only October. I think I would know if it were the weather."

"Alright, let us calm down, lower our voices, and talk this out."

"Ah come on boss man. I am dying of thirst over here." Dex groans, practically falling over onto my shoulder.

"You will be dying of something else if you do not knock it off." Doc bristles, advancing upon the inebriated analyst with her ladle of death.

"Enough!" I snarl, desperately clinging to my last shred of patience. Both parties freeze immediately, taken aback by the unusually serious tone of my voice. Given my history, I do not favor giving outright commands, but I am not above playing the alpha card if it keeps this festival on track.

"Doc, I understand your concern on this matter, but those kegs were carefully watched and kept under lock and key. Also, Dex has had enough to choke a horse and he is fine. Drunk, but otherwise unharmed. Correct me if I am wrong, but there are no known ailments that could kill a lycanthrope through toxicity, short of pumping them full of silver. Since we would surely know if the keg was contaminated with that much silver, we can rule that out."

Doc nods in agreement with all that I have said. With the good doctor temporarily appeased, I turn my attention to Dex.

"Dex, my friend, you are extremely drunk. Go find Annie and eat a bit more before drinking more ale. We would not want to hog it all and leave none for our guests, would we? Doc is only looking out for you."

Dex offers no complaint at my words. Though Doc still looks worried, she gives one final nod of recognition.

"Both of you, please try to relax now. This is a festival! Enjoy some well-deserved time off."

"I suppose I can try." Doc relents.

"That is the spirit!" I pat her appreciatively on the shoulder and finally get myself some of Gus's famous ale, made specifically for lycanthropes. With the drama dispelled, for the time being, Kiro and I make ourselves comfortable in the fighting pit, though he seems hesitant to let me place any bets without having seen what the contenders can do first.

Time for some well-deserved, mindless spectating and a bit of gambling.

Swimming later? Kiro asks.

Sure. I am glad you are finally getting into the swing of things.

Within seconds, my mind is pleasantly consumed with Kiro's overwhelming urge to fish a pumpkin out of the lake and demolish it without mercy.

Seven

Finally, a calm second alone with Sela.

"Tell me what he was like when the two of you were young."
I plead, desperate to pick the brain of the female lycan who has
somehow become my sister by association.

Sela lets out a soft laugh, the kind of laugh that turns your
cheeks rosy pink.

"As a child, my brother was every bit the same as the man
you know and love now."

"Did he always want to change things, for your people I
mean?"

Sela's slim, well-defined features darken to a more serious,
shadowy hue. For a brief moment, I worry that I may have upset her.
Then, Sela responds in a soothing tone that lays to rest any fears I had
of troubling her.

"Actually, yes. Although, I will admit his ambition grew in
intensity after the death of our parents. Sometimes that ambition of
his can be...costly."

"He told me about the friend you lost. Kal seemed remorseful
about what happened but he did not tell me anything specific."

"Talia. Her name was Talia."

"Would you hate me if I asked what happened and why Kal
feels so responsible for Talia?"

"A few decades ago I would have said yes. I suppose time
gives even the most rigid of creatures perspective. Not even the hearts
of the most battle-scarred lycans can withstand the march of time."
Sela sighs listlessly.

I smile back at her knowingly, somehow having understood
that she was referring to Andre. Since Kal came into my life, despite

every truly horrible tragedy that has befallen me, I have found a strength that I never thought I could possess.

We are so alike, you and me. I think to myself fondly.

"Talia's pack was one of the many small packs trying to gain a foothold in the Americas when a cell of distant relatives belonging to the Russian prime family, who were heavily removed from the bloodline, arrived to seize control in the newly formed states." Sela begins to explain.

Her tone, which was so serene moments ago, has turned grim and forlorn.

"I am sure my brother has alluded to how things work in our world. The prime families control entire regions, which sometimes include multiple continents. Therefore, as the world expanded in terms of humanity's reach, we lycanthropes expanded our reach into new territories as well. To maintain their bloodlines, the primes allow smaller packs to operate individually within their territories."

"Wait, I do not understand how that helps their bloodlines." I interrupt.

"The smaller packs supply a specific commodity necessary for bloodline extension and diversification: females."

"Wait...you mean?"

She cannot mean that!

"Yep. They sell or trade their daughters for land, wealth, or additional protection from the Order."

The very mention of that vile organization still sends cold shivers up my spine.

I will make the Order pay one day for all that they have done to me and my people. I will free my race, and Kal's too...somehow.

"So, Talia..." I prompt Sela to continue with her tragic tale.

"You guessed it. Talia was born to one of these smaller packs within the startup prime's territory. She was raised to be sold off like a broodmare to the prime alpha of the newly founded American territory, which was completely imbalanced before the Brazilians declared their territory's boundaries."

"That is dreadful! No one should ever have to *be* with someone that they do not care for."

"That is not the worst of the situation. If you have the misfortune of being paired with a prime, you have one purpose in life. Should you fail to fulfill that one purpose, or resist in any way you die, or worse."

"I may regret asking this, but what is worse than death?" I ask, my voice trembling like a baby deer in the dead of winter.

"Beatings and starving are the obvious answer, but some primes have been known to get creative. These clever primes let the females they imprison develop intense attachments to someone or something, then the prime uses that attachment to control the female."

Obviously? How is any of this obvious? Such cruelty should not be obvious to anyone. No wonder Kal feels compelled to change things...I can see what drove him to kill those men. Non-violent or not, I do not think I could have walked away knowing what they did and what men like those primes are capable of.

I find myself feeling guilty for having been so hard on Kal, even if I did not express the fleeting doubts that flooded my mind upon hearing what he did to his father's former packmates.

"I realize that what I have said is a lot to take in, but this is just the beginning of Talia's story. I will ask once more, are you certain you want to hear this?"

I nod despite the sour feeling in the pit of my stomach. Like it or not, I need to hear what this poor girl endured leading up to her untimely death.

"Talia knew her fate from the beginning, as most of us do, and she was determined to escape. She probably would have too, but primes like Stefan, the one who rose to claim the American territories, do not play fair. To make matters worse, the one lycan I could think of that was strong enough to face Stefan, was nowhere to be found.

All of that is a moot point for now. Talia fled her pack days before the primes were set to come to get her. She used money that she had gathered doing odd jobs over the years to charter a ship to Europe."

"But she never made it?" I ask sheepishly.

"No, she made it. However, as I said before, primes do not play fair."

"You play fair." I remind her, trying to lighten the tone of the conversation.

Sela flashes me a brief smile of appreciation before continuing her story.

"Rather than cut their losses, Stefan and his knuckle-dragging goons came after her, determined to reclaim their property. Luckily, back in those days travel was a lot slower. Horses and boats were still the primary mode of transportation for all continents; and, with her head start, Talia was able to put quite a bit of distance between herself and Stefan. She also assumed that they would cut their losses rather than sink money into pursuing her. Instead, the American's made a point of pursuing her. By the time Stefan finally caught up with Talia, she and I were fast friends. The two of us bonded rather quickly because I was missing my brother."

"Where was Kal?" I interject.

"Honestly, I could not keep track back then. He was always traveling."

Despite the tragic nature of Sela's story, I find myself smiling. Nothing makes me happier most days than hearing Kal talk about his travels.

Sela does not share the sentiment. Like me, her brother left her behind without meaning to. Kal let his ambitions and dedication to his people get in the way of his relationship with his sister...she and I are so much alike that it is almost frightening.

"In any case," Sela continues, "when the primes did come, I was not about to let them take my friend. I convinced Talia to fight rather than run and contacted Kal, by letter, for help. I had hoped that Talia's ferocity backed by the strength of two seasoned primes would be enough to deter Stefan. When Kal failed to show up, it was too late for me to turn around and tell Talia to run. You see, I made a huge deal about running not being the answer because no matter where she would run, they would always chase her. If I had just let her run maybe she would be alive today. In the end, it was as much my fault as Kal's that she died...it just took me a while, and the advice of a lycan far wiser than myself, to see that."

"The fault does not lie with you or Kal." I offer reassuringly, knowing that my sentiment will not ease Sela's pain.

"We may not have been the ones that killed her, but our hands are not clean. Ellesse, our lycan history is so stained with blood that all our pelts might as well be red." She concludes.

"If this world were just, we would all be stained red with the blood of those we have wronged." I point out.

"I am sorry about your home." Sela apologizes after a moment of pensive silence.

"Kal is my home now," I inform her with a smile. "And so are you...if you want to be that is."

"I would be honored to call you my family, though I am still sorry for all that you have lost," Sela replies earnestly.

"Do not be sorry. I would not have all that I do if not for what I have lost."

The sound of urgent footsteps interrupts our heartfelt exchange. Sela's almond eyes darken to a stormy intensity, her dilated pupils fixing on the source of the footsteps as they approach my back.

"Sam?" I turn to address the anxious lycanthrope and find that his face is ghostly pale with a strange, rigid calm.

"Has something happened?" I question, alarmed at the tension of his ominous aura.

"I need her to come with me. You should go to Andre now." Sam addresses Sela, ignoring my inquiry.

"*You* have no authority over me. Kal may trust you, but I do not. Let us not forget that you played for the other team not long ago and could easily have killed Ellesse. If she is going with anyone, it will be me." Sela snarls defensively, placing herself between Sam and me.

"Kal sent me to take her somewhere safe." Sam protests through gritted teeth. Though his recently discarded humanity still shows in his facial features, Sam's brief time as a lycanthrope has already added an animalistic edge to his appearance and aura.

Sela bristles, looking feral enough to rip into Sam like a dog ripping into a steak.

"Sela." I place a soothing hand on her shoulder. "I trust Sam. Do not forget, I am the one who saved him. Something tells me he is not keen on seeing me die anytime soon. Besides, Kal would not have sent anyone if he could be here himself."

She turns and searches my face, puzzled by my last remark. Something in my features must convey the worry I feel inside, for Sela's features soften and she nods knowingly.

"Sela," I murmur in a hushed tone, unsure how much I can say in front of Sam. "find Kal for me. I have a bad feeling. As I said, he would have come himself if the situation permitted. I will do as Sam says for now and see if I can ascertain what has happened."

Sela silently agrees, then turns back to Sam who is none too happy to be stuck waiting on us.

"If you harm my new sister in any way, or I find that you have been dishonest you will wish for death," Sela warns, glancing worriedly in my direction one final time before departing with unnatural speed.

Sam turns his attention to me, his sense of urgency making me anxious. "Hurry now," Sam instructs as he helps me to my feet, "we are not safe here, they could be..."

"Sam, I agreed to come with you, but you need to tell me what has you so on edge. What could be so bad that Kal would send you specifically rather than coming himself?"

"I was told explicitly not to say any more than necessary. All that I will say is that Kal was safe when I was sent to get you, but something happened in the glade."

117

We should never have left the glade. This is my fault. The only reason Sela and I wandered so far was because of the way I feel about fighting.

Sam grabs me by the arm and pulls me in the direction of the rocky slope that forms one side of the valley, running like a spine through the trees to form the wall of both the valley and the glade. The closer we get to the sloped wall of earth and stone; the tighter Sam's grip becomes.

"Sam...your grip? It is starting to hurt."

"Sorry." He responds without looking back at me. Sam's shadowed eyes remain fixed desperately on the terrain in front of us.

That is enough! I cannot handle the tension in his aura anymore.

"Sam!"

He whips around and covers my mouth with lightning speed.

"Ellesse, we have to stay quiet now. I know you are upset and do not understand what is happening, but I know little more than you do. I am just trying to keep you safe as instructed. They could already be here..."

Mid-sentence, something small and blindingly fast-moving hits Sam in the back knocking the wind from his lungs. Sam's hand slips from my face, blood flowing from the corner of his mouth, as he lurches sideways. For a gut-wrenchingly tense heartbeat, Sam struggles to stay on his feet before grabbing my arm again.

"S..Sam?" I stammer.

Just as he recovers, Sam is struck a second time by another tiny projectile. This time I hear it coming. I attempt to deflect the fast-moving object, but my wind is not strong enough, nor are my reflexes sharp enough, to match the projectile's speed and force. The impact of the second unknown object pushes Sam forward.

"Sam!" I struggle to hold him up, searching for a place to hide from the unseen source of flying objects.

"Gunshots. Those were silenced long-range rounds." Sam groans, producing tiny rivers of blood from his mouth as he speaks.

"Guns cannot hurt a fairy. Kal told me so himself."

Now knowing what we need, I reach out with one hand toward the closest tree and encourage the scrawny thing to extend its limbs and roots. As the tree shifts into place, forming a protective barrier around us with its twisting limbs, Sam speaks again.

"Ellesse, normal guns will not kill you, but a gun with iron bullets could certainly kill you as you are now. Rifles like these can fire many shots in rapid succession before either of us gets anywhere near the source. That many wounds…the blood loss…you could die even if the bullets are not iron." Sam pants, his chest rising and falling in a clear sign of pain.

"Let us not worry about the specifics right now, Sam. Just sit down and try to heal I suppose." I instruct frantically as I attempt to clear my head. "These bullets, will they hurt you?"

"My reduced healing and the familiar burning sensation suggest that these bullets are silver. So I will not heal. However, the bullets missed my heart so I should live. I should probably work on removing them." Sam pauses then raises his head as though he has just thought of something important. "You are connected to all living things, correct? Any chance you could locate the shooter?"

"Perhaps. I am dangerously low on energy. However, we are in luck; I happen to be the one fairy who can sense anything both on the earth and in the air."

"Excellent. Try searching to the South. I am pretty sure that is the direction the bullets came from."

My hand shakes as I place my palm against the frigid earth, spreading my fingers out like a star as I reach into the sparse grass. For several tense heartbeats, I feel nothing but a steadily rising fear within myself. Then, gradually, I find my center and the plants begin to speak to me in a way they only can for faeries and other earthbound species.

I just need to keep it together long enough to get Sam out of here and find Kal. If I can manage that then everything will be fine. I tell myself, struggling to maintain my calm.

My eyes drift slightly to the heavily bleeding lycanthrope lying on the ground beside me. Droplets of cold sweat bead across his forehead and drip slowly down his face like sap dripping down the trunk of a tree.

"Do not strain yourself and do not worry about me. Remember, I have been through worse." Sam smiles, referencing our initial meeting.

I smile at him gratefully. "True enough. You were in very bad shape that day. I cannot believe it has only been a few weeks."

As I speak, still trying to locate the creature with the gun, Sam fishes the first bullet out of his side. He pants heavily for a moment before reaching back to try removing the second bullet from his lower back. Before he can make much progress, Sam freezes, his nostrils flaring slightly and his narrowing suspiciously.

"You can stop now. I know you are tired. Besides, I can smell them."

"Them? There is more than one? What are they and where?" I question nervously, breathing heavily from exhaustion.

"Lycans, no doubt about that. There are two I can sense at this moment. Each is approaching us from a different side of the tree, one to your back and the other to your right. Any chance you could buy me a little time without sapping what remains of your strength? Whatever you do, avoid losing consciousness. I may need you to run."

If he thinks I would be so cowardly as to leave, then he has not heard my story.

"How much time do you need? I can buy a bit of time, but I make no promises."

He nods. "Just do what you can without going too far."

Sam returns to the task at hand, digging his nails into the wound in his back to pull the bullet out. Unable to watch such a bloody act, I turn my focus to deterring the rapidly approaching lycans. With the two lycans closing in I can sense them on the grass with less resistance than before.

They are practically on top of us! I feel myself panic. *The fact that they have not chosen to shoot us yet means that neither of them is the one who shot Sam. As if we needed any more problems right now...I suppose all I can do now is slow these two down with the only weapon I have at hand.*

With my connection to the air strongest in Kal's presence, I opt to go the other way and utilize the roots of the tree we are sheltering under. The mani in my arms burn immediately upon pouring my ani into the ground beneath the tree. The strain of what would normally be an effortless task for a fairy of my caliber is immense. My hands and feet tingle after only a fraction of a second, as though they are being pricked by a thousand tiny needles. Despite the tremendous strain, I manage to give a silent command to the tree's roots to attack the approaching lycans, as a bee would attack a threat to the hive. My task complete, I slump over wearily, the edges of my vision blurring.

"Did it work?" I ask between labored breaths.

"It did. I should be able to heal now; I managed to remove both bullets. We will wait three seconds to let my wound start healing, then we make for the slope."

"Sam. As close as they were, I do not think either of them had the gun you spoke of. If they had guns, I am sure they were the tiny ones that fit in your hand."

Sam smiles again. "Those are pistols and I agree. That is why we will need to move quickly." Sam pauses again. "Shit. Your plant trap missed one."

"That can happen. If I had enough energy, then I would have used cyclones."

"That would have been entertaining." Sam grins briefly before going deadly silent. He rises into a crouch, then creeps, as slowly as a sloth, around the tree, raising a palm to indicate for me to stay put.

I hold my breath as best I can, but my shaky breathing remains frighteningly audible.

If I cannot find a way to silence my breathing, then they will find us for sure.

I can hear my heart pounding like a drum in my sensitive ears as the seconds tick by, passing as slowly as if they were hours. These molasses-slow seconds form the longest, tensest moment of my life.

Why did it have to be a full moon tonight? By the time we manage to deal *with the one my root trap missed, the other will have recovered.* I realize grimly. *If* *only Kal were here right now.*

My internal moment of panic is interrupted by the arrival of the lycan from my right, the one my roots failed to delay.

Shit. Sam, I hope you have a plan.

Luckily, though he cannot hear me the way Kal can, Sam has been watching carefully. He cleverly anticipated the point of the Asian lycan's arrival and positioned himself in the branches above. As the ill-fated lycan moves into position below Sam, the still-recovering former soldier drops down upon him like a mountain lion. In one swift motion, Sam tears a chunk from the throat of the thinly built lycan. He then follows up the motion by puncturing the man's chest, with a single, devastating strike.

The slender, somewhat short man reaches up to clutch his throat and finds only a void. He opens his mouth to speak or scream and where once there was sound there is now only blood. Clutching desperately at his chest, the man goes deathly still. My first impulse is to reach forward to heal the unfortunate creature, but I know better. Even if he could be saved, he would only come after Sam and me. Still, watching the man choke to death on his blood as his damaged heart slowly fails, is not something I was prepared for today.

"Are you ok?" Sam asks as though he has not just killed another creature with his bare hands.

The young lycanthrope quickly pulls the body of the other lycan, whose name I will likely never know, behind the closest boulder and covers him partially with dirt, branches, and shreds of root left behind in the scuffle between the lycanthrope and my root trap.

The poor soul fought his way past one danger only to die by another.

All I can do is nod in acknowledgment of Sam's question. I do not judge him for what he had to do. If anything, I blame myself for putting us in this position.

I just wish that no one had to die today. I suppose I should expect such a mentality from Kal or Red who have known nothing but violence, but Sam...was human only a few months ago. Are all creatures so violent? I wonder, losing myself in philosophical thoughts.

"We need to move." Sam pushes me gently toward the slope. "Can you run?" He asks worriedly as he examines my face.

Again, I nod, this time swallowing hard as I regain my composure.

"Good. When I say so, run as fast as you can toward the slope." Sam instructs.

My pulse quickens again. The base of the slope is a solid twenty-five meters from where we are now, and I am too drained to even attempt flying.

Calm down. Even if those bullets are special iron bullets, and Sam said they were silver, I know they are there now. Knowing the bullets are there means I can dodge them if I focus. So long as I can avoid being hit in the heart or head, I can likely heal using the moon. I just have to make it to the slope, and I am safe. I can do that. I tell myself encouragingly.

"Now!" Sam growls abruptly, shattering my thoughts.

I take off as fast as I can manage without the use of wind to propel me. After only a few strides, my sides are lanced with white-hot pain.

Not a bullet. Just exhaustion. I tell myself, struggling to remain calm. Such feelings of painful exhaustion are alien to me.

How far we faeries have fallen. I lament, fighting back tears of anger and frustration.

As the slope grows painfully close, I catch a glimpse of Sam out of the corner of my eye. Though he had seemed to be right behind me, at some point the nimble lycan must have turned and run in the other direction.

Sam, what are you doing?

For another eternally long second, time freezes like the surface of a pond in the dead of winter. Even the pounding of my heart and white-hot pain in my side seem to disappear.

Any second now I will hear that awful whirring sound and Sam will be...

The thought of Sam taking another bullet on my account is more than I can stand. Without thinking, I stop running, sliding awkwardly in the dirt. The pain in my side comes rushing back, stronger than before. My vision blurs once more, my peripheral vision darkening ominously. I wait for the horrible noise, fighting amidst a sea of pain to make my way back to Sam, but the noise does not come. Rather, Sam's tortured voice rises over the pounding of my heart in my ears.

"No! Do not stop, you need to run! I will be fine." Sam's cracked voice calls out to me.

As my vision clears, like a heavy fog dissipating in the late morning, a second shadowy figure appears behind Sam.

Oh, holy hell...is that...Feng?

"Looks like my intel was good after all. Who would have thought that the great Greyback would shack up with a teeny tiny fairy?"

There is no mistaking that arrogant tone, even from this distance. That is definitely Feng, which explains why Sam was so keen on getting me out of here. The question now is how Feng discovered who I am.

"Leave her be," Sam growls defensively.

Feng turns his attention disdainfully to Sam, who refuses to budge from his position between us.

"I did not expect to see you among the living. What was your name again?" Feng sneers coldly.

What a piece of work. I may have felt a pang of sympathy for your cause before but what you did to Sam was unforgivable. I stew bitterly, wishing I had the strength to send him flying or bury him alive.

Feng continues speaking to no one in particular, ignoring Sam as if he were little more than an insect.

"How is it you are even alive? Surely there was enough bane in that ale to fully disable even a new lycan's healing. My little trick certainly worked on the blonde-haired one; I doubt we will be hearing from that guy again in this life." Feng laughs cruelly, having amused himself.

Dex. The twins are the only two blondes around here and Feng referenced a male. If he is talking about Dex that means he has been to the glade or the manor, perhaps even both.

Anger sets in alongside my panic. Having my home invaded once was bad enough, repeating the experience is not something I care to endure.

Something about Feng's words does not compute for me.

"Sam...what exactly happened before you came to get me? Why would he be talking as though he has been in our home? Did something happen that I should know about?" I question, trying to keep the panic from my shaking voice.

"Looks like the clever bitch is figuring things out. Oh, in case either of you gets any clever ideas, the one who shot you is still watching. That business with the tree was an annoyance I do not care to repeat, so my underling does have instructions to shoot the fairy in the head if either of you tries anything."

"Sam, answer me! What is he talking about? Is my family safe?" I demand again.

"Do not listen to a word he says. Feng is a master manipulator; you cannot trust his words. Remember, no matter what, Kal would never lose to *this* wolf!"

Feng tires quickly of Sam's words. In a single, swiftly executed motion, the prime slashes a deep line horizontally across the center of Sam's chest.

"Sam!" I scream without thinking.

Droplets of crimson blood fly in a fanning arc from Sam's chest, landing on the ground as silently as if they were little red doves.

Since when can Feng do that? He just sliced into Sam with only his hand. Something like that is only possible for wolves like Kal who can partially shift body parts. I realize.

"Enough! Sam has nothing to do with this. You came here for me, so leave him be."

Feng throws back his round head and roars with over-dramatic laughter. Such a chauvinistic gesture makes me want to vomit.

How lucky you are that I am out of energy at this moment.

"Ironically, you are right. The runt has nothing to do with this. He is, however, in my way."

Despite his rapid healing, Sam's blood loss has taken its toll. He now sits, doubled over on the ground to Feng's right.

"Of course," Feng continues in his condescending tone, "he does not have to be in my way. As you pointed out, I am here for you. I cannot make any promises regarding the fate of your friends at that little gathering of theirs, but I can still let Sam here walk away from all this unharmed. Rather, *you* can let him walk away. All you have to do is come with me quietly." Feng states calmly as he casually strides closer to me, passing Sam without so much as a glance in his direction.

"You are a monster." I am too numb to bother putting hate into my words. Instead, the statement comes out a void, emotionless, fact and is met with a triumphant grin.

"I have news for you, fairy girl, we are all monsters, yourself included. That is why the mewling humans are so determined to keep us contained. They just cannot handle being anywhere other than the top of the food chain, which is ironic given the number of non-humans that eat them."

"As a fairy, I respect the natural order more than any creature; however, not all humans are attempting to suppress us. Most humans live their lives blissfully ignorant of our existence, like sheep in a field. Would you ask a sheep not to fight for its life when faced with a wolf? No creature wants to live its life in fear, you are proof of that. What you seek to do, inciting violence, will only lead to massive loss of life on both sides."

"That might mean something if it were not coming from a fairy. Your species has done nothing but hide while humans destroy the world for the last three thousand years. You are perhaps the most cowardly race there is, even more so than the dragons, assuming they still exist."

Dragons? Does this wolf have a head injury?

"Easy for you to say. Your species has no need to worry about a pair of large wings upon their backs or pointed ears that give them away wherever they go." I retort bitterly. "Such big talk coming from a ruthless killer who would see us all fighting to the death over the most insignificant infractions. Sam mentioned the methods you utilized on the newly turned humans...those that survived the initial transition and subsequent starvation."

"Just our way of culling the weak and keeping those that remained in line." Feng shrugs.

Sam is right; there is no chance in the hell nor on earth that Kal could lose to any lycan trained under this brute. I tell myself hopefully. *I just need to buy myself some time until he can find me...and he will find me. Kiro could find me anywhere. That clever wolf may even know what I am feeling and thinking as we speak despite my weakened state. The trouble is cooperating enough to keep Sam alive in the meantime...*

Having guessed my intentions, Sam speaks. "You cannot go with this bastard, Elle. He will kill you and have me shot for the hell of it."

"You know, I am starting to lose my patience," Feng growls, his face contorting into a menacing snarl baring pointed canines in a grisly reflection of the rabid wolf with whom he shares his mind. Even without having seen Feng's wolf in the flesh, I can tell the monstrous beast is nothing like Kiro.

Feng steps back, turning his attention to Sam. He lifts Sam by the neck with ease, clearly using his wolf's monstrous strength in his arm and hand. With a series of sickening pops and snaps, Feng's free hand morphs, in a dramatic show of force, into a hairy, clawed version of a human hand. Where once there were nails, now rest curved claws, and a black pad now replaces the light skin of Feng's palm.

"Enough! We get it. Now put Sam down. However, I will not move from this spot until I see the man with the gun. I do not trust you to keep your word not to harm Sam."

"So be it. Just know, if you so much as mildly irritate me, I will see to it that he dies, along with everyone else back in that valley."

Technically this is part of the valley, you moron. I think to myself angrily.

Feng callously drops Sam, as though he were little more than a doll. He then steps casually over Sam, who is still gasping for breath after Feng's near throat-crushing vice grip.

Oh lovely. This is going to be fun.

Eight

Why can I not stop staring?

"Brother...say something! God damn it you drunk asshole! Please, just say something..."

Why can I not speak?

"Don't you dare leave me, you insensitive moron! You cannot just leave me here..."

Dex.

What remains is barely recognizable. More than half of Dex's blood soaks the ground beneath our feet in the formerly lively valley glade, staining the earth a grotesque shade of deep crimson. Dex's formerly blonde hair is now black with rapidly drying blood, his features a ghostly pale shadow of their typically carefree state. Already his eyes have dimmed and sunken, retreating into the formerly handsome face of a man I considered as much my brother as Sela is my sister.

Annie kneels beside her brother, understandably distraught. The thin framed sharpshooter looks so small and pale beside such carnage. She struggles to process what has happened, clutching the front of her brother's blood-soaked t-shirt so fiercely that the knuckles of her trembling hands turn bone white. Annie's distraught screams turn rapidly to shrill shrieks of pain, drawing the Brazilians in like a bug light.

"Why did he not heal?"

"Was his heart damaged?"

"What of the security system? We were assured of its quality."

"Wasn't he just in the pits? How did he get way over here?"

The gathered crowd devolves into confused questions and bristling accusations.

"All of you be still!" Carlos snaps.

"Annie…" I approach the unstable lycan cautiously, knowing firsthand what grief can do to a member of our species. "I realize this is unimaginably difficult to process but try to sift through what you are feeling now. Whoever did this…"

"Will die slowly and creatively while screaming for mercy until I cut out their damn tongue!" Annie roars, her eyes manic and devoid of all emotion except rage.

"If that is what it takes to calm you, so be it."

"We are so far past calm Kal…" Annie turns to snarl at me.

"Annie!" I cut her off. "Have you forgotten so easily what I promised him? You were always his only concern in life Annie. Dex is…or rather, was my brother but now we have to focus on how this happened and how we stop it from happening to anyone else."

I turn my attention to other matters before Annie can enrage herself any further. "Sam! I need you to find my sister and Esse. They wandered off a while ago and I do not want them alone. Send Sela back here to me and get Esse as far from here as possible until I have located whatever did this."

For a moment, Sam hesitates, not having seen carnage like this in some time. Then he meets my gaze and nods, understanding that if he fails to find the girls in time, they could be the next to meet this gruesome fate.

Sam pauses before turning to leave. "What if Sela will not listen to me? She and I are not exactly on great terms given my…history."

"I do not think it will be a problem. Esse knows me better than anyone and she will question why I am not there instead of you. Her concern should be enough to convince Sela. If you must, simply imply that Andre needs Sela. She has never been one to refuse Andre when he requires her assistance. Now go and avoid making yourself a target."

Sam wanders off leaving the rest of us to sort out the events that led to such tragedy.

"The rest of you, our priority is to determine what..."

My words are cut short by a distinct whirring thunk, and a dull gurgling cry from one of Carlos' men, who promptly doubles over. The man hits the ground with a resounding thud and twitches slightly before going motionless.

Is he...?

Dead. Kiro answers my thought before I can finish it.

Shit.

"Everybody scatter! Take cover now!" Carlos and I shout in near-perfect harmony.

More whirring ensues as bullets fly left and right from too many sources to count offhand. With at least half a dozen rifles unloading on the valley full of half-drunk lycans, chaos ensues, bringing with it the stench of gunpowder and blood.

From the corner of my eye, I catch sight of Chiron and Andre as I dive into the tall grass of the hunting fields. The vibrant-winged fairy desperately attempts to provide more cover for the crowd using the sparse foliage of the glade. However, Chiron, having spent his strength to prepare the gathering place for the festivities, is unable to produce much cover.

A glance toward the Brazilian from the first shot confirms that he is dead.

Can you tell where he was struck?

He was not shot in the heart or the head. Kiro observes, confirming my worst fear.

We should have listened to Doc. I realize solemnly. *We must proceed under the assumption that none of us can heal.*

Esse. All Kiro can think about is the endless string of possibilities by which Esse could be dead or dying right now.

She is with Sela. The two of them are extremely capable females. I am certain they are safe for the time being. We do not even know the target of this attack yet with certainty.

Sela...Kiro's strategic mind refocuses, and worry takes root in our shared consciousness.

Shit. You are right, my friend. We sent for Sela without knowing the gravity of our situation. If she returns now, she could walk straight into this kill box.

Or try to stop it. Kiro points out.

That would be just like her. I agree. *We can only hope that Sela has not lost her street smarts. The Sela I know will be prepared for this.*

We wait in silence for several agonizing seconds, scarcely daring to breathe. Then, movement. One of the injured Brazilians rises, in desperation, from his hiding spot.

Do not do it, you moron. Better to take your chances bleeding close to the earth than to get shot in the heart.

Another muffled gunshot and the poor idiot hits the ground. Dead.

Damn it. He should have just stayed put a bit longer. This cannot continue forever.

We cannot sit here waiting to be picked off like fish. Kiro agrees.

I think you mean fish in a barrel but that is beside the point. If Doc was correct, then the toxin stopping our healing was in the ale. Are there any among us who did not drink?

I cannot be certain. Kiro whines in defeat. *Chiron?*

Not an option. He is tapped out. I doubt even Esse could save us now after depleting so much of her energy. Still, we should make our way over to Chiron.

Risky. Kiro points out.

A risk we will have to take. He is not looking so good. I observe. The glowing green hue of Chiron's arms is visible even from my position in the tall grass. Esse's mani glow in that same hue whenever she exhausts herself.

Fine. Kiro relents, sensing my unease. *We crawl slowly.*

I send my stubborn wolf a silent signal of gratitude as we begin to crawl in an agonizingly slow pace, on our belly, through the tall grass. We crawl two body lengths or so before Kiro gives an urgent warning to stop.

Too much movement. He warns.

Sure enough, a single bullet impacts mere inches from my right leg followed by another half a foot from my hip and one final bullet centimeters from my left ear.

Lousy shot. Kiro remarks pointedly.

True enough, but they are certainly determined enough to put holes in anything that moves.

After several seconds of somewhat patient stillness, Kiro gives the all-clear for us to move once more, slowly and under the cover of a slight breeze.

Excellent. Moving slower than a snail is exactly what this situation calls for.

Do you want to live or not? Kiro remarks, criticizing my impatience. *Better to arrive late than not at all.*

When the hell did you get so educated? I growl internally, grateful to have a wolf like Kiro.

Chiron spots us as we breach the edge of the tall grass. The seasoned fairy looks pale and frail, even his wings are drooping and dull with the strain of his efforts.

"Relax. You have done enough for us." I call out to him as loudly as I dare without drawing attention to our location.

Chiron nods his chest heaving slightly. "I tried to protect them. I am just...too drained." He pants, leaning against the thin base of the tree serving as his only means of protection from the deluge of bullets.

"You did all you could, Ki. Just rest now. Any chance you know whether or not these bullets are iron?"

Chiron's brow furrows and his eyes darken with sorrow. "Iron or not I wish I could give you better news. If Elle is as drained as I am, being struck by one of these bullets could do some irreparable damage. However, as her second I can tell you that both of us would know if she were dying or dead."

"What do you mean?"

"Well, you now possess the link that she previously maintained with the keystone. As her second, Ellesse and I have a cultivated telepathic connection that, physically, works as a two-way connection."

"Wait, does that mean you know *everything* she is feeling?"

Chiron grins knowingly. "Thankfully no, though in each other's presence we can read body language and basic thoughts. Elle and I can also send messages to one another long-distance, but it takes a lot of energy, more than either of us has at the moment."

"That is a shame. Your telepathy would be handy right about now."

"One thing I never understood," Chiron mumbles, trying to keep both our spirits up with a conversation. "Why did those nuns not use guns. You have said bullets can be made from iron at a higher cost, but the nuns had money."

I stifle a morbid laugh at the memory of that horrific day. "Ironically, the Order relied on the poison to bring her down not the iron. If they had used the bullets, then we might not have been able to save her unless Oberon's power can remove shrapnel from a body with surgical precision."

"A mistake they are not going to make again I am betting." Chiron sighs.

"Do not worry about that now. Just focus on surviving this first."

"What if we do not make it?" Chiron muses morbidly.

"If no one comes to bail us out of this, and I do believe Sela will come, then I will claw my way out of this valley myself and take as many of these bastards with me as I can before the blood loss kills me." I declare, trying to sound upbeat for Chiron's sake.

"Then they better hope we never make it out of this valley." Chiron smiles faintly before slumping back into the red earth below.

Though my bravado was meant to keep up Chiron's spirits, there was genuine intent in my words. The reality is, if neither Chiron nor I make it out of this valley, there will be no one left to look after Esse. Leaving her all alone in the world is not an option for me; therefore if I must sacrifice myself to get Chiron out of this I will gladly do so.

"Kal." Chiron's voice rouses me from my depressing thoughts.

"Yes, Ki."

"I feel movement."

Shit. This is it. They are moving in to kill off those of us who remain.

"How many?"

"Too many."

"Well do not sugar coat it Ki," I growl.

"No, I mean too many for these men to be the gunmen."

He is right. I recognize these men.

Care to let me in on the secret Kiro.

Before Kiro needs to answer me, a familiar voice calls out.

"Please tell me you are not dead yet Greyback."

"Ivan! You beautiful bastard!" I call back.

Ivan appears over us, extending a hand to help me to my feet, his most elite lycans already assessing the damage and taking stock of the dead.

"How did you find us?" I ask the grizzled Russian prime.

"Your pistol of a sister." Ivan indicates toward Andre with his chin. Tending to Andre's single gunshot wound is my savior of a sister.

"Kal!" Doc's tortured voice raises clearly above the clamor of wounded lycans, halting me in my tracks before I can thank my sister.

"No time for pleasantries then." Ivan shrugs as calmly as if he were vacationing at the beach.

"Doc I am here," I call back as we drift hurriedly toward the source of her cry.

"Tell me she is with you!" Doc cries as we come into view around the overturned stone table closest to the fighting pit, which she was using as a hiding spot.

"Doc who…" The acrid stench of blood hits me squarely in the face, churning my stomach and stinging my eyes. On the other side of the table lies Gus. Blood saturates the gentle giant's back, staining his ivory t-shirt a dark satiny red. In another place and time, the color would have been eerily beautiful.

"Doc, I…Esse is not…I am sorry."

"Do not tell me sorry, Kal, fix this!"

The image of Dex's bloodied, ghost pale face flashes through my tormented mind and I find myself feeling just as I did the day that I slaughtered my father's remaining pack. The rage is indescribable.

"Ivan."

"I am here." He answers.

"Get me your medic and a volunteer to give blood."

A morbid smile creeps across the old tyrant's face. "I believe I can do that Greyback."

"AB neg is Gus' blood type. Any donor will do." Doc murmurs, still trying to stem the flow of blood from Gus' multiple gunshot wounds using her t-shirt.

"Doc, I will take over now. We need tubing and a needle; in case the medic did not bring them."

"Right. That is right." She nods, her hands shaking uncontrollably as I switch places with her.

"Doc now!" I snap with all the ferocity of a rabid dog after she fails to depart. "I have no desire to see another brother die today."

Doc hurriedly scrambles away as instructed; her posture reminiscent of the days following her arrival at my door when she was still little more than a battered hostage.

So begins, once more, my descent into darkness.

"He did not know about the ale. When the shooting started…after Dex…I guess he was just afraid I would not heal. Lycans were dropping like flies around us and there just was not enough cover close by. When the fighting mounds deteriorated, we made for the tables. He…Kal, he…" Doc begins to stammer, her eyes shimmering with the promise of more tears as they fall upon Gus' broken body. Though he is stabilized, for the time being, his labored breathing still suggests that Gus is not out of danger yet.

"When you failed to reach the tabletop in time, he used himself as cover," I conclude grimly.

Doc nods, her tears now falling once more upon the back of our most jovial and gentle-hearted lycan.

"Carlos." I turn to the still seething alpha who has joined Ivan, Sela, and a slowly recovering Andre in the clearing behind the stone tables.

"How many of our men remain?" I ask.

"Our dead number six in addition to the young analyst. Only eight of my pack remain now, including myself and Andre. We will fight." He concludes defiantly, his brother, Julio, among the dead in the valley.

"Doc, how long until our healing is back?"

"That depends on the consumption and the relative strength and metabolism of the individual. I would say another three hours for the majority. Gus had the most, aside from…"

"Aside from my brother." Annie steps forward to join us carrying a carefully wrapped bloody package. The thin, weary female clutches the package protectively, as though her very life depends on its safety. All present in the clearing bow their heads slightly in respect, recognizing the parcel to be Dex's heart. With Dex having no one in his life besides Annie, the two of them were near inseparable. Losing Dex is as hard for Annie as losing my father was for my mother. Though Annie has always scoffed at tradition, as have most of our family, this one tradition gives her hope that Dex will remain with her in some small way.

"When Gus has healed, we will know it is safe to hunt the bastards down who did this," Annie states coldly. "And I want to be there."

"Yes." Doc nods. "Once Gus has healed all our healing will have returned."

"We should administer the tests to be safe before selecting the trackers," Andre interjects.

"If this is the Order?" Sela chimes in worriedly.

"Nothing changes. Order, lycans, does not matter to me. This will be answered." I declare to solemn nods of approval.

"We should send for Esse, now that the danger has passed," Sela suggests.

"Already done," Ivan responds. "One of my trackers was dispatched the moment you mentioned her. I cannot have Greyback losing his will to continue." Ivan declares pointedly.

"You have my thanks for that." I nod.

"Boss!"

"Speak of the devil!" Ivan grins. "What have you got for me, Sacha?"

A thin well-muscled Russian lycan steps forward, a bloody figure leaning against his shoulder.

"Sam?" Sela gasps.

For a moment I fail to process what Sam's solitary return to the valley must mean. Then, Sam spells it out for me.

"I could not stop him...he can do that strange thing you primes do. I swear I did not know he could do that. He never let us see..." Sam struggles to speak, clearly suffering from heavy loss of blood, despite the rapidly healing nature of his wounds.

"Sam, you are not making sense. Are you saying a lycan did this? Where is my Esse?"

"Kal, it was him. Feng did this...he has her."

Sela and Annie turn to me, looks of despair creasing their faces. Sela is the one who finally speaks, seeing that I am unable to process what Sam has said.

"Feng has Ellesse."

Nine

Feng. . .has her. My Esse.

We kill him now! Track him down and kill him. Kiro's rage has reached a dangerous new height as his thoughts turn to little more than murderous images of him ripping into Feng like a pinata.

In all my years sharing a mind with him, I have never known Kiro to be this murderous. He is no longer able to form coherent thoughts or complex sentences.

Keep it together, I may need your senses.

Nearly overcome by rage myself, I turn away and pull my cell phone from my pocket, my body operating as if on autopilot.

"Kal. . ."

"Sela, just don't right now." I snap, unable to put forth the energy to address any of their concerns. My mind is endlessly berated by images of my worst nightmares come to life. Esse with her throat ripped out, Esse torn in half and all other manner of horrid means by which Esse could perish.

She has already been with that creepy Asian bastard for too long. How long has it even been? I wonder.

By now, Feng has had plenty of time to reach a vehicle. Even if he traveled at speeds under the legal limits, he could potentially be anywhere.

If I do not find her soon. . .just keep dialing. I tell myself.

After dialing the desired number, the phone rings three times before a familiar voice answers on the other end.

"Kal, your timing is impeccable as always. We need to talk."

"Later Don. He has her."

Don goes silent, caught off guard by my right-to-the-point tone.

"Feng?" Don finally asks after what feels like several minutes but is likely less than a second.

"Yes."

"I am on it." He assures me.

"Don. It's time."

"Are you sure that is what you want? Are you ready?" Don asks, his tone calculated, without any trace of nervousness.

"Completely," I assure him.

"I will make the arrangements. And Kal, I will find them. You have my word."

I do not bother trying to respond to Don's reassurances. The words would not come even if I had the energy or time to respond. Thankfully, Don needs no further response; he hangs up without another word.

"What was that about? Kal what did you mean by it is time?" Sela questions.

Andre's stern hand on her shoulder silences my sister's string of questions. For good measure, Carlos throws Sela a silencing glance.

"Sam, I need to see the place where you last saw her."

"I can show you." Sam starts with a grating tone.

"Do not trouble yourself. You are too injured to do much more. I will go alone. Everyone else needs to stand by and focus on recovering. Just point me in the right direction."

"Think again boss." This time it is Annie who speaks. "This bastard has taken everything from me. You cannot ask me to just sit and stay on this one."

"That goes for me as well," Doc adds. "Before you protest, consider the fact that Annie and I have had the least to drink of anyone here and are both unharmed. Besides...we will just follow you if you do not bring us along."

"She is right," Annie adds. "How can we ask the world to change for us if we are not willing to change with it."

"Besides, I cannot sit here and watch him bleed anymore. I just cannot do it." Doc cries, turning to Sela with a desperate look in her eyes. "As the only one of us left here, can you please stay with him for me? Make sure he knows that I am safe because of him."

Unable to refuse Doc's anguished plea, Sela nods. "I will stay."

"I think you better accept their offer Kal. These she-wolves do not strike me as the type to take no for an answer." Carlos growls, a hint of amusement creeping into his otherwise dismal tone.

"Then we leave now. Keep up." I relent, still trying to hold Kiro at bay.

The two females, determined to see this through with me, nod and rise to follow.

"Should we gather weapons?" Doc suggests softly.

"No need. Sam says Feng par-shifted. Pretty sure the cocky little prime is going to be unarmed and I doubt he thought ahead enough to bring any of his remaining men with him. Besides, I would bet my life that he is not expecting two female lycans with your skills to come at him." I hope the last bit will boost Doc's spirits. She could be vital to our success today.

"So you want me to use the sight then?" Doc asks.

As an omega, Doc retains the unique ability to see into the near future in a limited capacity. Though all omegas retain slightly different abilities, Doc has managed to inherit two distinct bloodline gifts: foresight and flesh stitching. The second ability is a strange technique that utilizes Doc's strength and allows her to heal small wounds using her own body as a means of transferring some of the damage from the creature she is healing to herself. This secondary ability is one she has not mastered yet and fears deeply. If done incorrectly, the flesh stitching technique can leave both the omega and their target unable to heal at all. Though Doc still has a long way to go before she can repair massive wounds with her abilities or predict how someone will die twenty years from today, she has progressed rapidly since being freed from captivity.

"Not yet," I respond. "I need some idea of what direction they are headed in. Then we find where they got into their getaway vehicle, which Don should be able to find if it is a rental or stolen, and that is when you will do your thing Doc." I explain as we move quickly in the direction Sam indicated. Following his blood trail is easy enough.

"I see. You need me to get you a plate then?" Doc infers.

"And a location if you are able. Do not over-exert yourself. If all you can get me is a vehicle make and model, that will be enough for me."

"You can do it Doc," Annie encourages, "you are as strong as any of us. I know you feel like you hide behind Gus, but none of us, not even Gus, think that about you."

I smell them. Fishy Asian mutts. Kiro snarls hatefully.

In addition to the distinct smell of Chinese lycan, the smell of blood grows stronger as well, setting Kiro's already agitated state into overdrive.

If he has done something to her...

More rabid thoughts ensue, clouding my mind and senses.

Kiro you must calm down now before we lose control of our body. Do not make me have Annie knock us out. What will losing control do for her now?

Reluctantly, Kiro eases back into the corners of my mind that serve as his domain.

See, the blood is all Sam's and that of the lycans that pursued them. Besides, Esse has her trump card, the one Chiron told us about back in Canada.

She does not know. Kiro objects.

Based on what Chiron said, she does not need to know.

For reasons no one in the fairy race seems to understand, Ellesse was born different than all other faeries. She is not just different because she is a guardian; Ellesse is rumored to be some sort of cursed child with powers and strange abilities beyond her control.

I first witnessed her odd abilities one day when she and Kiro were swimming in a tiny pool of water by a waterfall. As a result of some prophetic occurrence beyond my understanding, she fell; falling should be impossible for a fairy given their ability to self-correct like a

143

cat when close to the earth. Though they can fall from the sky, faeries can never trip and fall while on the ground. However it happened, Esse fell that day and scraped her knee on a rock and the water responded to her without provocation, healing her injured leg. Even Kiro felt a strange pull, as though a voice in the back of his head was compelling him to help Esse.

Very strange indeed. The voice was louder than yours has ever been. Kiro admits, recalling the strange sensation of being drawn to Esse's side like a moth to a flame.

I am grateful to see him reflecting on more pleasant moments with Esse as he recalls the way he felt swimming with her that day. The last thing I need is for him to panic and go off half-cocked right now. Should we die, there will be no one for Esse to lean on when she does not know where she belongs or who she is.

There is still so much Esse does not know. . .

"I detect three." Annie interrupts my silent reflection with Kiro.

"You and Doc each take a scent trail. I will continue to track Esse's trail on the assumption that Feng went straight for her."

The two nimble lycans peel off in their respective directions to track their targets. As for me, finding the point of convergence between Esse and Feng's paths takes no time at all. The sparse terrain of this stretch of the valley practically does the work for me.

She left a calling card. Kiro observes as we come to a tree that has been altered by a fairy.

Based on the blood spatter, which Kiro confirms to be exclusively Sam's, Feng caught up to Sam first. Then, for some reason, Esse appears to have doubled back to them from nearly twenty meters away before exiting the valley along the same path as Feng.

Foolish. Kiro growls, frustrated by Esse's typically reckless behavior.

You know as well as I do that she would never leave Sam, or anyone else, to die.

"Hey Kal! You are going to want to see this." Doc calls out from a small crop of rocks just beyond the dip in terrain to the left of the twisted tree.

"Can this wait Doc? We are in a bit of a hurry here." I call back.

"You are *seriously* going to want to see this Kal. As in right now!" Annie, who has already reached Doc's location by the sound of her voice, calls back to me in answer.

So help me...

Enough Kiro. Trust in our family. I remind him.

"I am coming," I growl back in an unenthusiastic tone. "Would it not have been easier to just tell me what I need to see?" I question in exasperation as I bound over the dip and slide down toward the rocks, which are much larger than I initially estimated from my previous vantage point.

I approach the towering rocks with mild apprehension, having sensed a third set of vitals coming from behind the looming boulders.

It is injured. Male. Fishy. Kiro informs me in fragmented images.

To my genuine delight, Kiro is spot on. Upon rounding the far side of the ominous boulders, we find a male lycan in human form ensnared by russet-brown roots as big around as my legs. In his struggle to free himself from the death grip of the roots, the unfortunate soul has caused part of the rockface to collapse on top of his legs and stomach. Now pinned to the earth and slowly suffocating, the lycan will surely die if not freed.

"Well, I'll be damned if it isn't my lucky day." I snarl at the hapless lycan. "You are one of Feng's brutes. I see that you have met my fairy."

I kneel closer to the blue-lipped henchman to examine the roots and rocks that have bound him in place.

"Those roots look pretty sound. I take it they are fully intact." I inquire to the two females standing over the mystery lycan.

145

"They are some of her best work, all things considered," Doc confirms.

I turn my attention to the short, yellow-ivory-skinned lycan before me. "I bet you sure would like to get out of this little predicament. The only problem is, I would much rather see you stay right where you are. The same goes for those two lovely ladies; they are not thrilled at how you and your alpha have treated our comrades." I indicate with a tilt of my chin toward the two females standing behind me.

"Please. I cannot tell you where he is unless you free me. I can...barely speak." The man sputters.

"Wrong answer," I growl. With one swift, well-practiced, motion of my right hand, I par-shift my nails into hardened claws and dig them into the man's side between two ribs.

Gotta love par-shifting.

The poor bastard lets out a muffled, guttural scream, dark rivers of blood trickling from the corner of his mouth.

"I have neither the time nor patience for games and groveling. Either tell me what I want to know, or I just leave you to slowly die here as you deserve. One way or another, I will find him, and I will end him for all he has done. I would prefer to expedite the process as much as possible."

For good measure, I twist the fully formed canine claws clockwise to widen the rapidly healing wound in the man's side. Once more, he screams though the sound is heavily muffled by the lack of oxygen in his lungs.

"St..op!" He finally rasps. "I do not know exactly where he is just that he is in the middle of nowhere. A farm or something...on the coast."

"What was he driving and what direction was he going in?"
"North!"

"The vehicle." I press my sympathy for the plight of this pitiful creature before me all but gone in the wake of today's losses.

146

"He ripped off an old green truck. Makes a foul sound when it starts up." The man sputters desperately, coming in and out of consciousness now.

"Thank you for your cooperation," I state coldly.

With all the bedside manner of nurse Ratchet, I tear my claws free from the man's side. As his wound heals, the man slips into unconsciousness, the lack of oxygen finally having rendered him unable to maintain consciousness despite the full moon's light.

Pathetic. This is what had us pinned down waiting for death? We must be getting old. Kiro and I think bitterly in a strange unison.

We should kill him. Kiro suggests callously.

As if having read my mind, Doc interjects. "Kal, we are not them. We do not leave people to die...that just is not who we are. Besides, you are likely the only one besides Esse who can dispel those vines. His life, or death, is literally in your hands."

"You are right." I sigh.

Though I do not understand much of the strange connection I now share with Esse, the keystone's energy residing within my body seems highly responsive to my thoughts and impulses, making it easy to control. As Esse has done a thousand times, I place my hand against the agitated roots and picture vividly what I want them to do. Within seconds, the restless roots retreat into the soil.

Doc steps forward to remove the rocks from the man's lower body but I bar her path.

"He can get himself out from here. We may not be murderers, but I will not risk Esse's life to show kindness to those who wish us harm. We saved him, that is enough for now."

"If he knows what is good for him, the lucky son of a gun will make himself scarce the minute he wakes." Annie balks, none too happy about sparing someone she views as responsible for her brother's death.

"If he insists on causing trouble, you have full permission to vent your anger on him," I assure the fiery gunslinger.

"Doc, I think it is time for you to do your thing." I request, trying not to make my words sound like a demand.

She nods and wanders off to seclude herself so that she can focus better on the task before her. Foresight is not an easy gift to harness. While Doc does her thing, I dial Don. He picks up the phone almost immediately.

"Anything yet?" I gush before he can get a word in.

"Nothing concrete. I take it you have found me something more to go on?" Don muses.

"Green truck, old by the sound of things, makes a strange noise when started. Based on the info we think the vehicle is stolen. Also, possible location: farm up north by the coast." I fill Don in on the information we have obtained.

"I see. That is a vague description at best but let me run it."

"Doc is doing her thing as we speak," I inform him.

"Good. Let us hope she can get me a plate. That would help the process along."

We should track it. Kiro growls impatiently.

You know as well as I do that we would never be capable of differentiating the scent on a highway or even a secondary road. Even if we got lucky and they took backroads, our current method would still prove faster.

Not if you let me run.

Yes, that will draw no attention whatsoever; a wolf running up the road. What good would us being caught do for Esse? I question bluntly.

More waiting then. My impatient wolf huffs.

I do not like this either, but we have no other options.

Truthfully, I am every bit as frustrated and terrified as Kiro. Without Doc and Annie to keep me centered, I doubt that I would even be coherent at this moment. If events had gone the way I intended, Kiro and I would have run off half-cocked and let the lycan in the roots die.

"Boss!" Annie breaks through my self-reflection with perfect timing. "She is done."

"That did not take her long. Doc is improving."

"I am indeed. Got you a plate and everything! 182-D-13725. Also, Esse appears to be unharmed for the moment, but she is very weak. The house is small and definitely near the ocean as the strange lycan said." Doc relays her findings to me in an urgent tone, rattled at having seen Esse in such an exhausted state. None of the family has seen her in such a state before, other than Chiron.

"Don, tell me you heard that."

"I got it." He confirms. "Give me a second, plates do not run themselves."

"Hurry." I urge, feeling like a frog in a slowly boiling pot of water. I turn to the two females standing just behind me.

"Be ready to go. Doc you are driving. Annie, do what you do best. Oh, and pack a med kit with purified water." I instruct frantically.

The pair turn toward the slope leading to the manor and take off at full speed to prepare. I take the opportunity to reign in Kiro, walking pensively after them while waiting for Don's search results.

See, we already have a possible location and a plate for the truck.

She is alive. Kiro agrees. *I want her back.*

We will get her back. I assure him.

"Still there?" Don asks as we approach the manor.

"Of course."

"I hope you are ready. We got lucky this time and have a clear location." Don informs me as the girls pull up in Red's finest Jaguar.

Not the most subtle car in Ireland, but it will do.

As long as it is fast. Kiro interjects.

We will make it fast. I assure him. *Whatever it takes, we will get her back alive.*

Ten

"You have my word, there will be justice for Dex and Gus too," I assure a visibly tense Annie as Doc drives the last stretch of the twisted route to the location Don provided.

For the last few minutes of the drive, Annie and Doc are both silent. Then, as Doc brings the Jag to a stop on a dirt road leading to the location we marked on the map, Annie finally speaks.

"I know you will. That is not what is bothering me now." She sighs heavily.

"If you are worried about the effects of the bane, nearly an hour and a half have passed since then and you did not have much..."

"No, nothing like that." Annie interrupts, shaking her head. "I just...I am worried about the way I feel. All my life, even when I was young and alone in that mining tunnel, I never felt cheated. Sure I was angry, but I moved past the anger because I had Dex." She pauses, trying to bury the pain that has become all too familiar to each of us. Tough as always, Annie resumes her composure in the time it takes for us to exit the Jag and begin gearing up.

While Doc goes ahead on foot to scout out the tiny cabin-style farmhouse, Annie continues her thought.

"Not even the beheading of my parents phased me, certainly not the way it hurt Dex. I always assumed that was because I did not know my parents well. Now, I believe the real reason I never felt rage at the horrors of this world was that Dex was always there to make me smile. He was my twin brother, yet he seemed so much older than me and so much stronger too. I guess I just wanted to be strong like him. Now Dex is gone, and I am left feeling like...I cannot explain it."

"Like you could burn the whole world down?" I offer as I check the three pistols Annie packed as our primary weapons and the rifle she packed in case the opportunity for a distanced strike should present itself. Annie turns to me with eyes brimming with sympathetic sorrow.

"I forget that you have experienced such feelings firsthand. How did you do it? How does one get over this overwhelming sense of rage that threatens to swallow you whole? Sari has never been so angry or frantic before; she is a completely different wolf now without Dex and Theo." Annie confides in a rare moment of vulnerability.

"I did not overcome the rage. In the end, I gave into it; I burnt it all down." I admit humbly.

"But those men, they deserved to pay for the lives they took. Not just for your father, but all the lycans that came before him." Annie insists.

"That is the rage talking. Whether they deserved it or not is not for me to decide. What we are fighting for, means that no one, not even primes, will have the right to be judge, jury, and executioner. I am not saying I would not do it again; as Esse says, the choices I made back then made me who I am today. However, as Esse has also said, all life is sacred, and it is not our place to decide the value of any life but our own."

"That is one wise fairy. I forget how many years she has lived. Hard to believe that she has been around for twice as long as most of us. I guess that makes her some sort of cougar." Annie grins wickedly, resembling her old self for a fleeting moment.

A ghost of a smile flickers across my face. "Cougar or not she still looks like a child to humans. You should see the looks we get when we are not careful. I suppose I should be grateful she can even be in public." I sigh.

We go silent for a moment, waiting for Doc to return. Then, Annie speaks again, sounding more profound than she ever has before.

"Who even decides what is right anyway." She asks as she snatches up the scope for the rifle and fits it to the fine-tuned weapon.

"I suppose *we* decide." I shut the hidden compartment Red added to the trunk and close up the car before turning back to face Annie head-on.

"How about we make a deal, you and me. I will keep you in line if you do the same for me. With both of us looking out for one another, we can stay out of the darkness and always remember who we are and why we fight."

"Sounds like a plan to me." She replies, extending her arm.

I take her arm in my own and we stand, still as two statues in the light of the last full moon of fall.

"You two done chatting?" Doc appears from the nearby shrubbery, having finished her surveillance of the area. She boasts one of her trademark smiles, the kind of genuine smile that was so common around the manor kitchen before everything went to hell. Part of me wonders if I will ever see that smile in the same light.

"Yes, we are good to go. What do you have for us Doc?" I respond with an edge of amusement.

"Naturally, the binoculars were useless as he has drawn all the blinds and curtains. The sight has grown a bit hazy, but I managed to confirm their presence in the house. From what I was able to see, she is located in a small room in the back of the ground level. We have two entrances to the house and one into the room. There might also be a basement entrance, I could not make it out definitively." Doc explains.

"Doc, she has been in his possession for three hours. I have to ask, is she safe?"

"From what I saw of her, she is still as spirited and composed as ever. If anything, the little fairy is just exhausted." Doc assures me.

"Could you tell if she was glowing?" I ask, trying to remain calm despite the multitude of graphic images in my head.

"Actually, yes. Her veins seemed to be bright green, almost emerald."

"Those are not her veins. The faeries call them mani; apparently, the mani are channels that run through the bodies of most

152

creatures though they are vestigial in humans and certain other species, like lycanthropes." I explain.

"Remind me to brush up with my fairy anatomy when this is over." Doc requests.

"Annie, I leave it up to you to determine how we proceed with entering the house. If we can safely assume this is a three on one situation then we should have numerous options." I conclude.

"I believe I sensed an additional presence, but only one," Doc adds hurriedly.

"I still like those odds." Annie nods, turning to the items taken from the trunk. The strategist brought a veritable arsenal with her in preparation for multiple possible scenarios.

Before Annie can offer a sound plan of entry, the air around us grows tense with a strange pressure and sudden surge of electrical energy.

Big storm. Kiro informs me, his aura strangely nervous given the situation.

"There was no mention of any storms in this area today," Annie growls skeptically.

"Doc?" I turn to the omega for answers, but she shakes her head in confusion, every bit as baffled as Annie and me.

As the three of us stand in steadily growing tension and rapidly mounting confusion, the wind picks up forming an unusually strong, and eerily familiar, gale.

I know this. Kiro realizes. *This is her.*

Are you certain? We are on the coast. Strange storms whip up out here all the time. I offer, fearing what might happen if this storm is truly Esse's doing.

I am certain. Can you not hear them? Kiro insists.

Sure enough, through Kiro's keen senses, I can discern the cries of various animals. The rising chorus of anger and fear in the surrounding wildlife feels otherworldly, as though driven by forces beyond the comprehension of Earth's natural laws. Kiro's rage ebbs away and is slowly replaced by an overwhelming urge to protect. This drive to protect is no longer that of a partner but that of a creature seeking to protect its creator or, perhaps, its parent.

Kiro!

I am trying! He snaps, giving his best efforts to resist the strange magnetic pull.

"Kal do you know something about this?" Annie asks, her wolf suffering the same effects as Kiro.

"This is Esse. I do not know how or why but she has been pushed into a state of emotional unrest great enough that she no longer controls her power. She has subconsciously put out a call to both the elements with which she shares a bond to protect her in her time of need. This has happened before, though never like this." I explain, autonomously moving in the direction of the storm's epicenter.

The girls block my path, their wolves suffering lesser effects than Kiro, who is already predisposed to protect Esse at any cost.

"Look around you, Kal. No scientist is needed to know that this is not the kind of storm you just walk into." Annie pleads. "We promised to look out for one another and now I am calling you on it. Believe me, I know the things you must be feeling and thinking right now, and I know how badly Kiro wants to keep her safe but killing yourself is not the answer. Esse is like Doc and me. She does not need a savior; she needs a family. You cannot be that family if you are dead."

The desperation in Annie's voice is enough to give me pause. Even as she speaks, a bolt of white-blue lightning strikes a nearby tree to our right, setting the scrawny plant ablaze.

"The storm...it is too big." I find myself muttering like a mental patient. "She will be found if she keeps this up...or worse."

"Kal." Doc pleads softly, her voice a soothing, but trembling, croon, like that of a wounded dove. "Not even storm chasers would risk coming out in a squall like this. Not even the Order would be that reckless. The second the storm dissipates enough, we will move, you have our word."

They do not get it. The second the storm stops could be too late. All energy, even divine energy, comes from somewhere, and if Esse uses up all of hers...

Another tremendous jolt of white-hot lightning splits the earth a few meters ahead of us, between the three of us and the tiny house, sending up a violent spray of crystalized earth in a strangely beautiful geyser.

Perhaps there is a point to be made here. If the storm is this bad from several meters away I cannot imagine the effects of Esse's power up close.

We can make it! Kiro argues. *She needs us!*

Before I can attempt another protest with the girls, the stench of dense smoke drifts to us on the raging wind. Somehow we had not seen the black plume in the night sky. Over the house, a thick column of choking smoke rises to meet an equally dark cluster of clouds.

"That is it. We go now." I growl, unable to bear the mounting number of possible ways Esse could be dying inside that lonely little house.

I shove my way violently past Annie and Doc, not caring anymore if they follow or not. By now, the squall has begun to unload a deluge of torrential rain upon the house and the surrounding terrain. To my surprise, the two capable women follow me in accepting silence as I hurry into the sheet of rain.

"At least the rain will buy us time with the fire!" Annie calls out encouragingly.

"Even so, you two should wait here. The last thing we need is all three of us getting trapped in a burning house in the middle of a freak storm." I warn them.

Without further delay, I make my way around to the back of the small wooden farmhouse. What awaits me there I could not have predicted with a dozen guesses: A tree measuring as thick around the trunk as my waist has twisted its way into a gaping hole in the north side of the house. Splintered logs lay strewn about the ground, some burnt and smoldering in the pouring rain. As I pick my way through the wreckage, the twisted limbs of the tree grow thicker and more complex, centering around a single point in the center of what was once a tiny bedroom in the solitary farm cabin.

Though I cannot make her out with my own eyes, there is no doubt that Esse rests at the center of the protectively configured, cage-like tree. As I attempt to pull branches from the powerful yet ethereal cocoon, the tree continually regenerates with seemingly endless energy.

"Esse, if you can hear me in there you need to let your guard down. If I cannot get you out of this tree you will die from the smoke and flames consuming this house. You are safe now. Kiro and I are here. We brought Annie and Doc, and they are worried for you now."

The Great Tree. Kiro breaks his silence.

What about it?

This one is acting like it.

Kiro makes a good point. The Great Tree never behaved as though it was of this world. Even non-humans are bound by the laws of nature, though we can sometimes bend them to our will. However, the Great Tree was able to transcend the boundaries of death and behave as though it was both living and inanimate.

I do not understand how this helps us.

Stop fighting it. Do that thing you do with the energy from the rock. Kiro urges, as eager to free Esse from the rubble of the slowly burning house as I am.

I press my hands against the rough, damp bark of the tree and do as I did with the roots in the valley. With a single, silent request the tree pulls back a small section of willowy branches to reveal my little fairy curled up in a protective ball. Finally able to retrieve her, I find that Esse is cold and her mani no longer glow a vibrant green. Instead, the tiny unseen networks are now a dark brown-black hue, like some deathly omen. The intricate black lines swirl and weave their way up Esse's arms and chest to her neck and face, like creeping ivy.

Doc will know what to do. I tell myself.

"Doc! I found her. She is so cold…and she does not look so good." I bellow through gut-wrenching, smoke-induced coughs.

The torrential rains slowly dissipate, and the darkened clouds overhead begin to break apart as I drag Esse and myself from the smoldering house. Once clear of the wreckage, I collapse into the mud and wait for my eyes to refocus and my sense of smell to return after inhaling so much smoke.

How strange that I was so focused on the task at hand I did not notice how much pain I was in.

Adrenaline. Kiro agrees, showing his intelligence.

"Sorry Kal! We are here. Just had to go back for the med-pack." Doc clamors toward us and wastes no time in examining Esse. The good doctor does not need to speak for me to know that the situation is grim.

"You can fix this right Doc?" I murmur desperately.

"You are damn right I can," Doc growls back stubbornly.

See Kiro. Doc will fix this.

For the first time since finding Dex's mutilated body, I feel as though I can breathe freely. As with most good things in life, this respite does not last long. While Annie stands watch in case Feng managed to survive the onslaught, Doc's frantic movements, and desperate murmurings grow more manic by the minute.

"Doc, why is she not waking up? Did you try the water? She should heal on her own when exposed to the water under direct moonlight." I remind her.

"No need to panic just yet." Doc raises a hand to silence my concerned rambling. "We do not yet have all the facts. She is critically drained of energy. This may just take some time to work itself out."

"May? That does not instill much confidence Doc." I argue.

Kiro's memories flash back to the time he licked her wounds after scraping her knee. *The poor wolf feels every bit as helpless as I do. Centuries of training and study and we are useless when needed most.*

I am afraid all we can do is sit this one out and trust in those with gifts we lack.

"Doc, talk to me. I know this is probably a waiting game, but I need to know your prognosis."

"I think it would be best to take her to Chiron."

"That does not tell me much."

"I am not sure how to put this but, I think she is comatose."

Eleven

"Wings and claws aside, something has been bugging me since I got here, Chiron."

"So since the night before last?" The vibrant winged fairy retorts haughtily.

"Mock all you want, green wings, but I know full well that faeries feel emotions with the same intensity that lycanthropes do. I may not have ever met a fairy personally until now, but I have come across those who have in my travels. Furthermore, Ellesse may seem weaker than me at first glance but she is no pushover. If not for fate's intervention she would have knocked me into next week."

"Calm down. I understand. Believe it or not, I am older than Esse by just enough to have remembered the lessens our people teach on the subject of biology. You will have to forgive me if I am wary of your species' sorted history." Chiron scoffs, though he displays the faintest trace of amusement.

"Funny you should mention that. See, I have done my fair share of horrible things, but I still cannot fathom any set of circumstance that justifies sending a child off into the woods by herself to guard an old relic for the rest of her natural life." I snarl, none too happy at the idea of Ellesse having suffered alone for as long as she has.

"This is not for her entire life." Chiron counters, though the lack of confidence in his tone betrays his lack of faith in his statement.

"Fun fact about lycanthropes that you did not know; we can smell lies."

"I did not speak a lie. I merely told a half-truth. Let us clear the air about something; Elle is my family. I would gladly die for her, which is why I am her second. Essentially, she is my little sister. All of this is why she can never know what I am about to tell you. This entire millennia-long situation has been difficult enough for her, she does not need to feel unwanted on top of her existing doubts."

"She is not *unwanted*." I snap, snarling more aggressively than I had meant to.

"I see that now," Chiron responds with surprising calm. "I did not say she was unwanted, I said she feels unwanted. Just assure me you will keep what I have to say between the two of us."

"Only as long as she never asks. I will not lie to her."

"That will not be a problem. You will understand once you have heard." Chiron assures me.

"Fine. I still refuse to see what could justify mistreating her in such a way."

Chiron sighs, ignoring my comment as he begins his lengthy explanation.

"We faeries are connected to all living things, especially the living creatures of the biome we were born into. Certain faeries are born with additional connections to specific areas or objects of the earth. Our first king, known as Oberon, was born with an overwhelming connection to all of the earth. Everywhere he went, beasts of all manner followed and protected him. Furthermore, water healed him, the earth was said to shake when he was angered, and plant life would grow rampant in his very presence. No other fairy in our history has possessed such a connection to all things living. That is until the legendary siblings came along. Fairy king and fountain guardian, brother, and sister."

"Esse's brother is the king of the faeries?" I interrupt.

"Yes. Harlequin is the sixth fairy king. One would think him to be the more powerful of the two, and, at first glance, he seems to be the more powerful fairy. However, Elle displayed an unusual, eerily familiar, power at an early age. As a sprite, nature seemed to...*respond* to her."

"You mean the way it did for Oberon." I verify.

"Yes. Whatever Elle wanted, nature seemed all too eager to provide. When sad, the plants would produce flowers to cheer her up. Whenever she was scared, roots and vines would maneuver into a protective defense around her. Even animals seemed drawn to her. She always loved butterflies and often you would see swarms of them appearing to perform tricks for her, for no other reason than to make her smile. The worst were the rare occasions when she would become angry. Storms would form and wreak havoc until something, or someone could calm her down."

"These occurrences, she was never aware of them?" I inquire quizzically.

"No, she never appeared to notice these strange things happening even when they were directly before her eyes," Chiron affirms.

"And the storms would just stop when she cheered up?"

"That is also correct. Sometimes nature would take a turn for the worse and target the specific object believed to be the focus of Elle's emotions. One day, she conjured a storm so powerful it threatened to bring down the tree homes of her forest. Everyone just kept waiting for it to stop but it would not let up for anything. Her brother had to use Oberon to counteract the effects of the crazy weather. He nearly lost his life."

"So what; nature responds to her emotions. I do not see how that justifies the way she was treated. Why did your people not try and teach her to control her emotions and impulses the way we lycanthropes teach our children? From an early age, our children must be taught to control their emotions or risk losing control of their wolf and becoming feral."

Chiron shakes his head in solemn silence, releasing a heavy sigh. He shifts back into a sitting position on the branch in front of me.

"She does not realize what she is doing, Kal. She never remembers what happened even if we tell her about it afterward or present her with the resulting damage. If I did not know any better I

161

would say there is a completely separate side to her that she is not aware of."

"All of that warrants making her a prisoner?" I question skeptically. "What I am hearing is that this is a 'one for the many' situation."

"I do not understand what that means." Chiron raises an eyebrow at me.

"Do not worry about it." I dismiss coldly.

"There is more." Chiron insists.

"No shit Sherlock," I mumble.

"Who is Sherlock?" He asks in confusion.

"You have been living under a rock. I will explain later. For now, continue with the rest of your story." I urge.

"There were signs around the time of Elle's birth that indicated the influence of the divine. We call these signs harbingers. In Elle's case, the harbingers were all death-related. Furthermore, an affinity for storms is a rare and unique ability among guardians that is typically linked to anger and negative emotions."

"All of that is rubbish. I have known Esse for a few days and even I can see that she is as good as they come. Sure she may have the emotional stability of a teenager, but that can easily be attributed to the way she was treated as a child. I am certain growing up in isolation did not help either. If you all believed her to be cursed, sending her off to live alone, feeling unloved and abandoned, was the worst thing you could have done! I should know...I grew up alone and I barely managed to avoid going feral. Ellesse deserves so much better than this." I conclude.

"And I have to believe that she will find the happiness she is owed. That is why I am choosing to believe in what you have said. Maybe she is meant to be a harbinger of death and destruction, but it is never too late for someone to change their fate. You told me earlier that a dream brought you here to her. Perhaps that dream was something more. I have to believe that you are meant to put her on the right path."

162

Oh, the irony. Could someone as damaged as me even be capable of altering anyone's fate for the better?

Present Day

"I know this is a lot to ask Don, especially with everything else you have on your plate, but if you could find the time to contact Harlequin I would owe you so many favors." I implore.

"So long as you remember these favors once the dust settles old friend. You are racking up quite the debt here." Don sighs, though I can practically feel him grinning lightheartedly through the phone.

"This is all assuming I live long enough to see the dust settle." I groan doubtfully.

"Well with Feng burnt to a crisp your odds have improved. One less enemy to contend with and the final preparations are being made to end this three hundred year-long journey as we speak. Just hang in there a bit longer." Don encourages.

"I am just thankful Carlos is still with us. I would not have blamed him if he decided he wanted out given all that has happened to his pack." I sigh again, leaning against the high-backed, brown velvet, lounge chair that now rests beside the bed in my room. Tucked securely under the thick layer of quilted comforters and down blankets of our bed rests Ellesse, who has remained unconscious for the last thirteen hours despite our best attempts to heal her. My stomach knots upon taking in the stillness of her flawless face.

"Carlos understands the need for primes to leave behind the old ways and knew there would be heavy resistance and numerous losses." Don reminds me. "Kal, if you are not ready for this, we can still postpone to a later date."

"No. We continue as planned. There is nothing I can do for Esse right now and if I even think about Dex's funeral right now...this is the best use of our time. Besides, backing out now would show weakness and reaffirm the position held by Feng, portraying him as a martyr to the cause of our kind. Our species is divided enough, we need no further fuel thrown on that fire." I explain.

"I understand and I am glad to hear you thinking so reasonably given the circumstances," Carlos responds.

As things stand presently, I will have my hands full with the Italian and American primes, who both hold long-standing grudges against me and my cause. Each stand to lose much of their livelihood should the laws of the coalition of primes be instated.

With some luck, Andre can use his pull with the African primes to sway their vote. The African lycans are already far more progressive than the other continental territories. Australia is also fairly progressive so there is hope there as well...

"Did I lose you?" Don asks in response to my lengthy silence.

"No, sorry. I am still here...just thinking." I assure him.

"I should leave you to it then."

"Thank you again, Don, for everything. Do let me know if you reach Har."

"You have my word." He vows before hanging up.

Thankfully, the silence is short-lived as footsteps approach the bedroom door from the hallway leading to the staircase.

"How is she?" Chiron's trembling voice asks from the doorway.

"No change," I answer flatly.

"We can try the grand bathroom again tonight. I know it did not work before but perhaps her energy has had time to recover now after resting for so long. Perhaps we could even try the fountain pond in the main courtyard.

"I should have told her, or at least tried to warn her." I confide in Chiron without warning as I sink deeper into the inviting velvet of the chair.

"As I explained that day in the forest, telling her does no good. Even if she remembers she only sends herself into a hysteria-driven fit which triggers another event, thus, reverting her memory to before she was told. Do not…how does the saying go? Beat yourself up?"

"I should have at least tried." I protest. "Perhaps, coming from me, the explanation would not have been so difficult to process. She has that odd connection to Kiro; he could have attempted to show her…"

"Kal. You are not to blame for any of this. I told you that day in the forest that I believed in you. That has not changed and will not change. Besides, if the moonlight fails us, Oberon will surely succeed." Chiron explains hopefully.

"That is assuming we can get him here in time to use Oberon." I remind the optimistic fairy.

We both fall into an abysmal silence, contemplating the emptiness of a world without Ellesse in it. Everywhere she goes and everything she touches seems to make those around her smile.

"She will wake up." Chiron declares, breaking the dismal silence.

Unable to bring myself to speak, I simply nod in acknowledgment of Chiron's spirited declaration. After several pensive moments, I can no longer stand watching over the ghost pale shell of my little fairy.

"Can you sit with her for me? I hate to leave her but there is something I need to do so that something like this never happens again. I did not know it all those decades ago, but all along I have been fighting this war for her. I can only hope I have gone about this in the right way. As Esse has pointed out many times, morality is relative and the best we can each hope for is that our morality makes the world a better place in some small way. As much as I want to stay with her right now, I must prepare to finish this." I ramble, trying to dispel the trembling tone that holds my voice hostage.

"I understand, and she would too if she could speak now. Ellesse believes in you more than anyone. She believes that you hold the answer to the salvation not just of your species, but ours as well." Chiron replies.

"Thank you." I flash the weary fairy a grateful smile as I rise to take my leave.

There is no turning back now.

Having called for a meeting this evening after bringing Esse to the manor, the family, who are all staying in the manor tonight, have already gathered in the usual place. Always the early bird, Red is anxiously pacing at the bottom of the stairs when I arrive. The slender russet-haired lycan is the only non-prime that knows what is happening.

"You are going to put a hole in my floor Red."

"This is too soon." Red remarks simply.

"Red." I extend my arm to put an end to Red's worrisome pacing. "If anything, I fear that this has not happened soon enough. If I had only done this sooner so many of our loved ones would still be with us and Esse...well, you know. We will never feel ready for this, but the time is now."

I can see in Red's smoldering gaze that he understands, despite feeling uneasy at the sudden shift in momentum.

"Everyone is waiting as requested." He nods, stepping aside so that I can enter the media room.

The room itself is lit only by sunlight and the glow from the pinball machines, casting eerie shadows across the typically whimsical room. Gus's face is the first one I see, sitting under the watchful eye of our resident doctor.

"I cannot express how good it is to have you back Gus. How are you feeling?"

"Good as new, lad. How is our wee fairy doing? Ya know we are all worried sick over the lass." He inquires sympathetically.

"There has been no change." I fold my arms across my chest, subconsciously distancing myself from Gus's question. "However, that is not what I called you all here for."

Their puzzled faces give me pause.

I wish that my little family would all back out and leave me to face whatever comes next alone. This would all be so much easier if they would think of themselves for once. What comes next will only put them back in harm's way, but they will stick it out as they always have. No matter what I say or do, they are always there beside me.

That is what family does. We may have never had one before now, but I am pretty sure this is what it feels like. Kiro offers, revealing a touch of wisdom befitting a wolf of his age.

"I called everyone here tonight to tell you...to forewarn you, that Don and I have used our collective influence over the other primes, with the help of Carlos and Ivan, to call for an ingathering of sorts."

The puzzled faces of my family gradually turn white with worry. Doc rises first with Annie leaping up alongside her, anger brimming within her crystal eyes.

"You should have told us sooner! Please tell me this is not what you were talking about on that phone call? Have you been planning all of this without us knowing? For how long now? How much time do we have to prepare for this prime gathering thing? We do not even know who has filled in the role of Chinese prime alpha yet."

The ranting pours forth from Doc and Annie without mercy.

"I need data..." Annie adds.

"And my supplies. What if this turns violent?" Doc demands.

"Enough! Both of ya! Tis all arranged according to a protocol set forth by the original prime families more than a millennium ago." Gus cuts in, temporarily silencing Doc who glares at him with disapproval.

Annie, however, is not so easily pacified. "Absolutely not." She snarls rabidly.

"I agree." Doc declares more calmly, folding her arms assertively over her chest. "Knowing these primes they will rip you apart to 'symbolically take your power' or some other ridiculous tradition. This is just so soon and so risky."

"Calm down now. Like it or not, this be something the lad has to do." Gus scolds the two hot-headed women in a gentle tone. "As for you," Gus turns his attention to me, "this does not have to be something you do alone. Don't you know we are a family? Family does not sit back and let their family face danger alone; we look out for one another."

"Gus of course; but look what happened to you and to..." I still cannot bring myself to say his name. Dex has been gone only a few days I have not yet come to terms nor have I stopped blaming myself.

"Nothin' happened to me; I am standing right here. You know bloody well what happened with Dex was not your fault. None of us would be here now if not for you lad."

"What did I do Gus? I certainly did not do any favors for Dex or Annie." I growl stubbornly.

"Perhaps you should ask me before saying something like that. Do you think I would still be alive if you had not given Dex and me a new home with new identities protected under the reputation of the legendary Greyback? Sure, I am still angry but not at you. I would not have made it, even with my brother's help and you know that." Annie snaps.

"Do ya ever think about what would have happened to us if you had not taken us in?" Gus asks.

"Gus..." I try to protest but my strange little family does not give me the chance.

"Gus and I would have run, and for a time we might have been safe. But we would never have been able to stop. I would not have been able to embrace the part of me that makes me special all because that special gift of mine makes us both targets. Heaven help us if the primes had caught Gus and me; any pack but yours would have tortured Gus just to make me cooperate. We would have become little more than cogs in someone else's war machine." Doc explains.

"I would have kept on killing my way through life, trying to drown a pain that I thought could never heal," Red adds.

"I would have bled to death and left no one behind to remember me," Sam murmurs mournfully.

"Ya did not always make great choices or even the right choices, but the choices ya made led us here and gave us new lives. You are a chancer lad, and that spirit of yours pays off. Tis why we back you. We believe in you." Gus explains.

"I know you blame yourself because I tried to warn you and you did not listen, but you were only doing what you thought was best. Even if we had stopped the situation there, we would still be here now. The damage was already done." Doc reassures me.

Annie, having only just returned from her meeting with the ghouls arranging for Dex's pre-funeral processing and burial arrangements, offers her sincerest attempt at a smile. She and Doc, more than anyone else, should hate me, yet they stand as firmly beside me as they always have.

With a sigh, I lean back into one of the lounge chairs near the door, typically the preferred seat of Red.

"So there is nothing I can do or say to dissuade all of you from pursuing this with me? Even though this could mean the end for all of us if negotiations break down and my territory is absorbed or claimed by another prime?" I groan, knowing full well that I have been defeated.

"If this is what it takes to live...or die...free then yes, we are prepared to follow you right up to the end. I believe we have made clear that there is nowhere else for us to go nor would we want to be anywhere else but here. Our home is with this family." Doc reiterates.

I run a hand through my unkempt hair, feeling the weight of my eyes and mental exhaustion for the first time in nearly three days.

When was the last time I even slept?

Thirty-two hours ago. Kiro responds casually, having retreated into a resting state himself despite his best efforts to remain awake for Esse.

You might as well save our energy for the real fight. Kiro advises, having been touched profoundly by the kindness of our motley crew.

"I suppose if I cannot stop you, then the decision is made." I relent.

"Yep," Red confirms in his characteristically simple way.

"Then I suppose I should progress to the explanation of how the event will go down. I know that Gus is familiar with the process given his background, but for the rest of you, this explanation will be imperative to getting through this with all our lives and freedoms intact. To summon all the primes in one gathering requires that an offer of good faith be made as a form of collateral."

"What does that mean specifically?" Annie interjects worriedly.

"The good faith offer means that I have to offer the other prime alphas something worthwhile enough for them to come together for talks of a unified group, which we have just referred to as the coalition."

"What did you offer them?" Annie requests through pursed lips, her eyes narrowing suspiciously.

"The good faith offer is not important right now." I try to dodge Annie's clever line of inquiry, but she is too sharp for me.

Wrong answer. Kiro whines, shrinking away from the intensity of Annie's gaze.

"What they want is important to me. I am your strategist, so I need to know as much as possible. Now spill it or I will drag the information out of you." Annie growls threateningly, though her words are meant as a heartfelt reminder that we are only looking out for one another.

"I offered to step down as the Irish prime alpha and concede to the reclamation of my territory. However, the offer only needs to be fulfilled if the concerns of the gathering are not properly addressed." I assure the hotheaded sharpshooter hurriedly.

"Were you dropped on your head? That offer is so clearly a trap!" Annie exclaims.

"Obviously. Countermeasures have been taken. Don and I have spent decades preparing for this exact situation and so far the other primes are responding predictably. Trust me on this one." I assure her.

"What countermeasures? Be specific." Annie commands.

"Did you miss the part where I asked you to trust me? Besides, if we stop to discuss my countermeasures now, then none of us will get any sleep. Do not make me play the alpha card here." I plead with an edge of fatigue.

"Would it kill you to give me a few details?" Annie pouts with the very same degree of skill as Esse.

She has been giving them lessons. Kiro theorizes.

Gods help us if that is true.

"All you need to know at the moment is that we have a proposal on the table for the neutral primes: Japan, Africa, and Australia. The response to the proposal seems positive so far. With two of those three on board, we have a clear majority and no reason to fear the American prime's requested offer."

"Of course that bastard is the one behind your good faith offer thing." Annie grumbles. "You have not forgotten what he did have you?"

"Of course not," I affirm.

"What if these proposals are revealed to that jerk and he counters them with a better offer?" Annie theorizes.

"Give me a little credit Annie. I trust no one outside of this family; therefore, we anticipated word of the proposals getting back to that creep. Don has done his homework well and there is no offer the Americans could make that could counter those we have made. All

171

my adventures were not for nothing after all. For all this time, while I was gaining knowledge and fighting skills, Don was amassing a small fortune with the artifacts I acquired for him." I explain to the nervous strategist.

"What if this character hauls off and comes after you and convinces the other alphas to stay out of it beforehand?" Annie asks, always one to cover every angle.

"Highly unlikely. Tradition is sacred to the primes, more so to the original prime families like the De Santos family." I assure her.

"There is a tradition that covers violence?" Doc chimes in curiously.

"There are traditions for ever'thing," Gus informs her.

"Who enforces these traditions?" Annie asks, her voice dripping with venomous sarcasm.

"That would be the Bän," Gus replies.

"What is a bän?" Sam asks in confusion.

"Not bän with a lowercase b. *The* Bän. Traditionally a male, the Bän is the unanimously enlisted figurehead of the primes. He decides all ties on matters of concern, and he serves as a neutral authority for lower packs to turn to if they feel wronged. The Bän serves as the elected figured until he dies or steps down." I explain carefully.

"Am I the only one wondering who this Bän is and why he has not stepped in before to solves matters of absolutely abhorrent violence and injustice?" Doc rambles, losing her composure briefly.

"There is no active Bän. Fun fact, Kal's grandfather was the last Bän." Gus boasts.

Stunned silence ensues, falling over the room like a dense fog. Surprisingly, Sam is the first to speak.

"No wonder Feng wanted you out of the way so bad. He was right to worry with a bloodline like yours. I know my word may not mean much yet, but I think we should try to sit back and trust Kal with this. If someone like Feng feared you as much as he did then I see no reason why the undecided primes would not accept whatever offer you posed to them." The young lycan's words seem to pacify everyone, even Annie.

"Cannot argue with that." Red agrees, drawing surprised glances from the rest of the room.

"You know I have your back no matter what, right?" Annie sighs, shooting me a somewhat apologetic look. "But you know I am going to step in at the first sign of things going sideways."

"I would not have it any other way." I acknowledge, trying to accept the idea that my little family will be with me no matter where I go or what I do.

As it should always be.

✡ ✝ ✡

As night sets in, I find myself wandering the halls like some restless spirit. The rest of the family has long retired to their respective rooms, except for Gus and Doc who decided to spend some quality time together prepping for breakfast in the morning. While most of the family are still staying at the manor temporarily, Red has officially moved Annie into the manor permanently, per her brother's wishes.

Why did it have to be you Dex? You and Annie were not like the rest of us. There was never any blood on your hands. From the start, you were good, all the way to your core, and you never lost yourself. Even in death, you were such a joyful person. Perhaps it is for the best that you are not here in the coming decades. I do not know where our species is headed from here, but I do know that such a pure soul does not deserve to know the rage that comes next in facing our one true enemy.

I am perfectly docile thank you. Kiro interrupts, attempting to lighten my dismal mood.

Says the wolf who would have killed anything that moved thirty hours ago. I retort.

I had reasons. Kiro points out, referring to our shared desperate need to protect Esse.

You know that if you are not up for this, we can sleep in the office. I offer, knowing how difficult Esse's state has been for Kiro.

No. She needs us. He went to sleep.

Kiro has a point. We finally relieved Chiron, assuring him that everything would be fine with Esse for the rest of the night. The poor fairy refused to sleep the entire time he was watching over her for fear that something horrible might occur during his slumber.

So, as with the rest of our guests in the currently crowded manor, Kiro and I set up a room for Chiron just to the left of our own. Setting him up so close by allows Chiron, as Esse's second, to remain within range so he can sense when she finally wakes up.

You should go to sleep too. Kiro insists.

I send a silent acknowledgment of his concern and turn toward the stairs to return to the third floor. Once on the third floor, we make our way slowly down the hall, with Kiro assessing who is asleep and who is not as we pass each room. First is Carlos's room which adjoins the room where his only remaining brother is now sleeping. The next few belong to the men he brought with him. Far too many of the made-up rooms now lay empty; granted many more of them are now filled with Ivan and his pack, who have kindly stayed, along with Carlos, to prepare for the coming gathering.

I clench my fists as I walk, trying not to let my negativity seep into Kiro's mood. He is trying, with such determination, to remain positive despite the chaotic state of our world.

Next is Andre and Sela's room.

Andre...and my baby sister. I am so grateful now that Esse elected to put you both in the room nearest to our own.

With Annie staying downstairs in the room across from Red, everyone is officially accounted for.

Finally, I arrive at our room, marked by a large vintage door and simple brass doorknob. Taking a deep breath, I push the door open slowly, as though trying not to wake Esse from her sleep. The room inside is cool and dark, like a tiny cave. Inside, the room is filled with an assortment of potted plants, old paintings of houses covered in ivy, and a bookshelf stocked with leather-bound first editions that I have collected over the years. In the center of the room rests a grand, four-post, solid mahogany, bed with lichen green drapery picked specifically for Esse.

Nestled in the middle of the bed in a mound of pillows and silk bedding is my little fairy. As difficult as it is to comprehend, my entire universe now fits in that one plushy bed.

She is so peaceful.

"I wish you could speak to me now, Esse. More than ever I could use your wisdom for what comes next. Even if everything goes as planned, this will only be the beginning for us all. We still have the Order lurking out there, not to mention every other human on this planet that has a drone or camera phone. I never thought I would see the day when everything I had worked for was just a single step away. Now that the end of my journey is here I am beginning to realize that the fighting never really ends. All the times I told myself that everything I was doing would be worth it in the end, were little more than a meaningless farce. In reality, I was justifying violent actions and bending my morals by telling myself that I was above it all."

I sigh, sinking back into the chair beside the bed. Knowing I should sleep but unable to do so, I stare out the window over my right shoulder and search the moon for answers.

If only the answers to life's problems were that easy to find.

I find myself imagining what Esse would say if she could see me now.

Ridiculous. Kiro informs me, referring in his simple way, to the opinion Esse would hold of my self-pity.

"You are probably right," I murmur as much to myself as to Kiro and Esse. "Regardless of what you would say, I know that you would be honest with me, even if it hurt, my little fairy. Please wake up soon. I need you here. I know that just a few weeks ago I was all about keeping you out of this, but I realize now that sentiment was rooted in the ways of the past. Just because I want to protect you does not mean that I have the right to sideline you. So, I promise that if you wake up I will never dictate the terms of your involvement in this family's matters again."

Esse remains as still as ever, though I cling to the hope that she can hear my words. Exhaustion sets in rapidly as my eyelids become heavy and the dimly lit room and cool air lull Kiro and me.

Bedtime. Kiro demands once more.

Too tired to debate the matter, or even deal with my clothes, I curl up carefully beside Esse.

Strange smell. . .

Kiro is as observant as always. Emanating from Esse's shoulders is a strange woodsy scent that I cannot help feeling I have smelled before. I extend a hand to examine Esse and find something strange just behind her shoulder blades.

What the heck are these?

Feels like two gashes. Kiro answers.

"What kind of gashes do not leave any blood behind? Stranger still, why are there two parallel wounds where previously there was no injury?" I mutter aloud to myself and Kiro.

I fumble around for the light, my hands shaking. I finally find the switch and cut on the lights, turning hurriedly back to Esse. With great care, I sit her up just enough to examine the strange marks.

Is that silk?

The strange marks do not resemble wounds at all; rather, they bear more resemblance to a chrysalis. The skin just below and inside her shoulder blades is transparent and open, like a wound, but without blood or exposed tissue. Visible beneath the strange anomaly, are shreds of what appears to be silk.

Chiron will know what to do. Kiro and I reason almost simultaneously.

As I set Esse back down on the bed to call for Chiron, her dainty fingertips twitch so slightly that for a moment I doubt seeing any movement at all.

"Esse? Can you hear me little fairy?" I whisper desperately to no response.

Perhaps I did see what I wanted to after all.

No. Her vitals have changed. Kiro growls optimistically.

"Esse, if you can hear me, please come back now. Kiro is worried sick."

You are too! The anxious wolf snaps.

After what feels like an eternity, Esse's eyes flutter open. At first, she manages only to open her eyes halfway and utter a strange groaning sound. Then, slowly, her body adjusts, and her eyes open fully, her tiny hands finally able to form fists and relax on their own.

"Hey little fairy, it's just us. You are back at the manor, safe and sound. Do not try to move around too much just yet." I advise her, scarcely daring to believe that she is finally awake.

Initially, Esse stares up at me blankly, but her eyes slowly focus, and she smiles knowingly.

"Kal?" She looks around the room for a brief moment, taking in the familiar sight of the room she and I designed. "My memory is distorted. How long have I been asleep?"

Esse shifts to sit up before I can stop her and winces with pain as a result.

"Easy! These things just appeared on your back. I do not know what they are, but I was going to get Chiron to take a look. Now that you are awake I am sure everything will be fine." I assure her hastily.

"Kal." She smiles, one hand having ventured curiously to the strange markings on her back. "There is no need for concern. If I am correct, then these marks are the final stage of my wing formation."

Holy hell and gods above. We are so screwed.

177

Twelve

"Your wings...final stage of formation? I do not understand. I thought faeries wings started small and gradually grew as their muscles strengthened?" I stammer in confusion, trying not to sound unhappy or ungrateful.

"Kal I am hardly what one would call a normal case. The muscles that sustain my wings, and regrow them if necessary, are already fully formed. Therefore, my wings have grown in the same way they would if one or both original wings were damaged. As you would say, I am just special." Esse beams proudly.

I struggle to find the words to explain my muddled thoughts.

She has barely acclimated to living a normal life and now she will be stuck hiding in some forest again unless I can pay some magus to craft elaborate illusions for her every few days. How am I supposed to keep her safe and happy now?

We could take her to the Amazon. Kiro suggests.

But can we leave our people now? You heard the family today. No one lycanthrope can do this alone; we must face the coming threats together as a unit. We are so close to exacting real change in our world, a change that would benefit all lycans. How can I face any of them, after all that they have lost, if we decide to turn tail and hide? Dex, Annie, our parents, Sela...we owe it to them all to finish this.

"Kal." Esse's expression has morphed to one of loving concern, her eyebrows slightly furrowed but the ghost of a smile on her face. "Everything is going to be fine. Let this be a problem for tomorrow. For now, I am just happy that you are safe. What happened to Feng anyway? I take it that you beat him."

"Well..."

I think we should try and tell her. Kiro suggests confidently.

Do you have any reason to think it will go better for us than it did for her fairy family?

178

Yes. I sense something has changed. Just try.

"What do you remember?" I ask her calmly.

She eyes me suspiciously as she answers. "Feng did not let me see where we were going but he drove a noisy vehicle, not like the ones I have been in with you before. We ended up near the water. I remember that Feng was behaving irrationally..."

Esse's eyes narrow as she struggles to remember the events leading up to her summoning the storm. As Chiron said back in Canada, Esse's mind is attempting to prevent her from remembering, most probably to spare her the pain of seeing herself as a monster.

"He kept ranting about something," Esse continues, "something that was upsetting. Feng mentioned that he only needed *them* for the wolfsbane. He rambled on about getting you out of the way and then dealing with them."

"Them who?" I ask, my curiosity shifting temporarily from informing Esse of what she did, to finding out who Feng was working with.

"Humans. Feng was agitated because he had to work with..." Her eyes widen as my little fairy's memory catches up to her. "It was them, Kal; the Order."

"That slimy bastard. He had the nerve to give such a grandiose speech about fighting back against the humans, but when put down he had no hesitation in working with them against his kind. I cannot believe he would stoop so low and be so arrogant as to bring the Order down on our heads." Without thinking, my voice becomes a vicious snarling growl.

"Kal, I know you are upset and a bit scared, but we have been through this before. At least we have time to prepare. I am sure the Order does not even know what has happened yet or that Feng has failed...speaking of which you have not yet answered my question."

I should have known that I could not slip something like this past her.

"Esse, I am not sure where to begin. I suppose I should start by confirming that Feng is dead. You killed him and, in doing so, drained yourself so much that you have been in a coma for nearly two days."

Esse sits perfectly still, like a stunned little statue. Then, she reaches once more for the parallel rifts in her back, as though they might ground her somehow.

"That explains how the wings could be so far along...it takes days..." Her voice begins to break, trembling like a baby fawn in a clump of grass. "I just do not understand."

Kiro.

I am working on it.

She pauses again, her eyes focused on some unseen point in the distance. Presumably, Kiro has begun showing her the moments, as they passed through his eyes, leading up to the storm she summoned and extending to the present.

While Kiro does his thing, I slowly wrap both arms around her, keeping her close to me. After a few seconds, Kiro probes my mind, letting me know that it is safe for me to slowly proceed with my explanation.

"Esse, you know how I was always saying how special you are? I meant those words literally. You are extremely powerful Esse, so much so that as a child you somehow suppressed your knowledge of this power so that you could feel more normal. Sometimes, you do remarkable things without even knowing that you are doing them." I explain.

"So you have seen me do this type of thing before...you have seen me make a storm like that?"

"Kiro should be able to show you, but yes I have seen smaller instances before. While I was still, well, dying back in Canada you unleashed a tiny bit of your power against your brother. The strain of losing Bartro and nearly losing me was too much I suppose; I really would not know much about it as Kiro was the one who felt and heard what was happening. He could not see because my eyes were closed."

"He feels it every time?" She pries.

180

"Yes." I verify, have him show you.

Esse remains silent for a bit then sighs deeply, attempting to keep herself calm.

"How could these things have been happening while I was there? How could I have been so blind? I could have hurt people; I did hurt people. No wonder my fellow faeries feared me." Esse laments.

"Your fellow faeries are closed-minded traditionalists who locked away someone very special because they did not understand her. They are the reason this barrier exists in your mind. Do not concern yourself with their opinions of you. I cannot count the number of lycans who see me only for what I have done wrong, but that should not stop me from wanting to do right. Their opinions should not dictate what I do or who I am. The same is true for you. Now, on a more pleasant note, how cool is it that you and Kiro can pretty much share images in one mind now?"

"I have to admit, having a connection that goes two ways so vividly is amazing. I never thought, in all my centuries alone, that I would be this close to someone." Esse admits happily. "You never told me the way that he felt."

"Kiro's emotions are not mine to share." I remind her. "Luckily, he can share them with you himself now. You would not happen to know why this connection has suddenly deepened by chance?"

"Something to do with my wings I am sure. A fairy's power strengthens tremendously when their wings come in. Since Kiro is a wolf biologically, this likely gave us the connection we needed to communicate more thoroughly." Esse explains happily, her aura easing rapidly as our conversation turns to something easier for her to process.

"Now, we have some matters to sort out if you are feeling up to it."

She nods, signaling for me to continue.

181

"Are you certain Feng was working with the Order? If so, is there any chance they could know where to find you now?"

"I cannot be sure, but I do not think they know where to find us or have the means to bring us down. If they did, then they would have come for me by now without the need to work with Feng."

"Good." I nod, pressing my face into her hair.

"Kal, I have been thinking; it is only a matter of time before the Order catches up with each one of us. I am thinking that your people and mine could help one another."

"Perhaps." I agree. "If the gathering I am planning with the other primes goes well, then I am going to have more pull within the lycanthrope community. However, they would need a reason to believe in your people, and their ability to contribute to this predicament. Perhaps if the primes met Har and saw what he could do, we could convince them to work with him."

"Gathering of primes?" Esse pulls back just enough to look up at me.

"A lot happened while you and I were separated from one another. I made a rushed decision, one that I stand by. I called for a gathering of the primes. We just call it an ingathering."

"What does that mean?"

"The gathering is our final attempt to unite the primes, our end game. We intend to officially instate a coalition between the primes so that the violence will end, and we can focus on facing our true enemy."

"If the matter was so simply solved, then you would have done this long ago. What is the catch?"

"Sometimes I swear you are too clever." I laugh. "The gathering is a gamble of sorts. If I cannot convince the majority to agree or at least dispel the primary concerns of those gathered, then I could lose everything. All my rights as a prime would be gone and we would become fugitives."

"You say you stand by your decision. Therefore, I stand by it too. We will just have to make sure that you do not lose everything. Between the two of us, I think we can manage."

"You sound just like Doc and Annie." I grin.

"And Sela, do not forget Sela." She reminds me pointedly.

"In the interest of keeping you in the loop, I suppose I should let you in on the basics of the plan. Don and I have been working out a strategy for disabling the Order. The whole ordeal is complicated on another level, but we will present just enough of the plan, in written form, to convince the other primes that we have the resources and knowledge to take them on. You see, Don's true objective from the beginning has been to annihilate the Order. I do not know why he holds such a grudge against them, but he does. When he and I met and realized our goals could go hand in hand, we teamed up. The rest, as you know, is history."

"Your plan is a solid one. However, I need you to do something for me, something that will help your cause."

"Why do I get the feeling I am not going to like this?" I grumble in a low suspicious growl.

"Because we both know you will not like it. You need to take the credit for Feng's death. I take it that no one outside this manor knows the truth, so we need to keep it that way."

"Doing something like that makes me no better than any of them," I growl in an irritated tone.

"You are...comparing different fruit."

"Apples and oranges, my little fairy, though I suppose your version of the saying works as well. Esse, try and understand that I do not feel good about taking credit for killing someone as a means of inciting obedience in others. That is not the lycan I want to be." I protest.

"How do I put this? In the world you are building, such a perception will not take away from who you are and what you have built; you will be remembered for the good you have done not the steps taken to get there. Additionally, in this world that we live in now, the death of another prime at your hand will aid in the process of convincing the other primes to follow you." Esse explains.

"You are referring to the image of the Greyback's." I huff.

"Kal." There is now a pleading tone to Esse's voice. "I love you and I only want what is best for you and what I know will keep you safe. I have faith in you to stay true to yourself, despite needing to bend from time to time. Remember, we are working towards a future where lycans are no longer required to bend their moral code to get ahead in life, or even survive. Also, if you die, I die."

"You just had to remind me of that. I never agreed to such an arrangement. This is not a Shakespearean play." I point out with mild amusement.

"Too bad. This is just what happens when you fight to free women. We women turn around and do things that make you regret it."

"I would not have it any other way."

Thirteen

Esse's words ring clear in my mind as I pace the length of the second-floor banister, anxiously awaiting the all-clear from Don's third-party security to make my way downstairs.

I cannot believe Don has so many connects within the beast-kin community. Our cousins are certainly formidable guardians. That is probably why the Egyptians considered them gods.

Annie emerges from the stairwell leading to the ground floor. She stops as she reaches me, not bothering to turn toward me. We stand, shoulder to shoulder, with her watching the wall behind my back and my eyes fixed ahead on the banister leading down the stairs.

"Annie, did I go too far to get here? I tortured a man and nearly left him for dead. If not for you and Doc I would have left him for dead. In the process of pursuing something I thought I might lose, I seem to have lost myself. This is a dark path we are headed down. And now, I am about to lie to everyone, to play the role that I detest and be perceived as strong. How am I any better than Feng or Stefan? Am I just another monster? What if Feng and I are the same?"

"Honest answer." Annie prefaces. "Maybe you and Feng are alike in some ways. Both of you wanted what is best for the future of your people and had the ambition to back it up no matter the price. You just happened to come out on top. At the end of the day, I would not call either of you a monster. If pressed, I would certainly consider him more of a monster than you...for obvious reasons. He was a deranged bastard after all."

Annie pauses, then turns towards me with a thoughtful expression etched into her face.

"If there is one thing I have learned from stepping into this world of lycans and humans and things that go bump in the night, after spending nearly two decades hidden in a mining cave, it is that there are no heroes or villains, no good and no bad. What one holds sacred is, to another, sin. We are all just creatures trying to survive in an unforgiving world of cruelty and chaos. At our core, we each have something we hold dear, something that we would die for, and, if lucky, something we want to live for. Many of us have multiple of each of those things and even more things that we would trade our souls for. You, Kal, are no more and no less than Feng, for there is no measure of a life. At the end of the day, you were you, and Feng was Feng. The cards were dealt, and the die was cast. When the dust settled, you won, and he lost. None of us knows when or where our story will end or how we will be remembered. One thing we do know, my friend and my alpha, is that your people need someone to lead them now. That someone must be you, not because you are a hero, but because you are the one willing to put forth whatever it takes to make a lasting difference. So, do what you need to do now in the hopes that we can be better later. That is all Esse is trying to tell you by advising you the way she has."

Annie concludes her speech, clapping a hand against my left shoulder.

"Besides, you have me here and I vowed never to let you lose your way. In my family, in this family, we keep our oaths."

Despite my every gnawing fear, I smile, placing my hand where hers touched my shoulder.

"Annie, you are something else. Remind me later to make things up to Esse for being so stubborn and so hard on her. Oh, and to make things up to you too. Once this is all over, and the dust has settled again, we should all go to one of those fairs I have told her so much about, as a family.

"Sounds like a good time to me." Annie grins slyly.

And so, we begin our descent of the stairs, a little early, ready to face our fears and our dreams head-on, as a family.

✢ ✞ ✢

The atmosphere in the grand hall of the manor's ground floor is expectedly tense. Despite its size, the seemingly massive room is packed like a can of tuna with defensive, bristling lycans, each of which is incredibly dangerous. Upon entering the room, the welcome presence of Carlos is the first ally I identify. Next is Ivan and, of course, my own family who stand waiting for me at the front of the room. To my surprise, I also sense, discretely hidden somewhere in the room, the dilute presence of both my Esse and her guard, Chiron.

At least he is with her.

An amused sensation emanating from Kiro draws my attention temporarily.

What amuses you at a time like this?

They are in the banister of the upper level. Kiro informs me, his amusement stemming from the fact that they now possess the only birds-eye view of today's meeting.

If you are ready, I need you to read the room at all times. I remind my ever-dependable wolf.

Kiro growls his agreement, dispersing his senses through mine in a manner only achievable with decades of regular practice.

Red joins Annie and me, forming a protective barrier between myself and both aisles of the room, despite my objections to being treated like some dignitary in a foreign land. With everyone present, the three of us make our way down to the front of the slightly sloped room, drawing the attention of every lycan as we pass. Most of them seem shocked by my brazen decision to have Annie accompany me and Doc stand with us at the front of the room. A few lycans among the dense crowd seem angered by Annie's presence. The closer we draw to the platform at the front of the room, the more silent the room becomes until one could hear a pin drop.

Taking my place on the platform, with my family standing beside me, I give my long-awaited address to the gathered representatives of the lycanthrope community.

"You all know why you are here. This is the deal: we primes can squander what little time we have remaining fighting one another to the death over petty land and bloodline disputes, or we can set all that nonsense aside and address our true enemy. The Order of the Vatican."

The very mention of the Order draws instant tension and anger from the crowd. The first spear of resistance comes quick as a bolt of lightning from one of Esse's storms, from none other than Stefan, the American prime. My eyes light on Sela, who visibly tenses as the vile prime speaks.

"You expect those gathered here, wasting their valuable time, to believe you capable of dealing with the Order when far better than you have tried and failed?"

Here we go.

"I do not recall saying that I would take the Order on alone. No one holds the power to do that. But if any here wish to reap the rewards of my success in dispelling the threat of the Order, they will need to become part of the coalition of primes. Furthermore, you seem to have forgotten who you are talking to. I am the Greyback that destroyed his lineage with no pack, no allies, and no reputation as a prime. Now, I have all three of those things and more. I am sure even you can imagine what I am capable of now."

"Greyback or not, you are still just a welp who got his daddy killed and lost his temper over it. Why should any of us believe that same reckless child is capable of bringing down a cult of murderous humans that have plagued our existence for millennia?" Stefan sneers condescendingly.

"You speak as though you represent every prime in this room, a gesture of arrogance that I am sure is unappreciated amongst our fellow primes. If the others have concerns, I am here to address them." I remind the arrogant welp.

"What are you prepared to offer this coalition should the majority see fit to form?" Jafari, the African prime, speaks plainly.

I allow myself to smile. A calm, confident gesture that serves to thoroughly agitate Stefan.

"I am so glad you asked, Jafari. As I alluded to before, I would not dare waste your time by assuming I could solve your problems by myself. I am sure you all have heard of the infamous Don Drafe."

Restless murmurs erupt among the crowd once more.

"What I am sure you do not know about Don, is that he has connections, as evidenced by today's increased security. A security force, I will remind everyone, that was requested to ensure Order intervention would not occur today. Between these vast networks, which gives us lucrative pipelines through which to funnel weapons, as well as funding for travel, and Don's small fortune, we now possess the resources required to confront the Order. All Don and I lack now between the two of us is the support of our people. What is the point of confronting the Order if Don and I will ultimately die in some meaningless skirmish with our own kind one day?" I explain vaguely, withholding as much detail as possible to foster interest in the proposed unification.

"You would have us work as paid *dogs* for the beasts, who already think themselves better than us?" Stefan shouts with overemphasized disgust.

"Who said anything about the members of the coalition working for anyone? The primes protected within the coalition would be expected only to come to the aid of other primes in the coalition should the Order target them, thus forming a united defense against the Order. The only lycans going on the offense here, unless anyone else here desires to volunteer, would be myself and Don." I assure the critical lycans, instantly deflating the wind in Stefan's ego.

All eyes turn to Stefan, who has shown himself to be the primary antagonist to my coalition.

"Any further complaints Stefan? Or shall we vote now?" I prompt.

"I will never join ranks with a dog like you!" Stefan sneers, clearly having lost what little hold he had over the gathering.

For good measure, I heed the advice of my family and reaffirm my position in their minds, giving them a strong figure that they can relate to so that the other lycans will more readily abandon the old ways.

"You have the *nerve* to call *me* a dog? I kill dogs, just like I killed Feng. If you think for a moment that I am bringing this coalition into existence to hide, think again. I believe my reputation speaks for itself concerning my ability to deal with anyone who threatens me or my allies, and under this coalition, all lycans would be my allies. So, you are either an ally to the lycanthrope race, or you are our enemy. Choose wisely." I growl in a low, clear warning.

"I do not fear idle threats Greyback."

"That may be, but you certainly should fear me, Stefan. Regardless, I do not need to kill enemies of the coalition. Without protection or assistance from the rest of us, enemies to our cause will be picked off by the Order." I clarify.

I turn my attention to the gathered lycans, knowing I will get much farther with them than with Stefan.

"Can any of you in good conscious pass on this opportunity knowing it may never come again? Are you willing to condemn your sons and your packmates to more pointless death and needless hiding? Shall you and your sons be caged like lab rats or dissected? Would you see your bloodlines obliterated? Are you all truly so blind or so arrogant that you think yourselves able to survive when so many others have fallen?"

The primes begin eyeing one another, at first with the usual suspicion, then with intrigue. For the first time, they all seem hopeful that the day to trust one another has finally come again.

"You once called my grandfather, Ragnar the Grey, your Bän, though many here never knew those days. All I am asking for is that you trust me to bring forth the same peaceful coalition that he did."

190

"While taking away our rights to do as we please." The Italian prime, Gio, interjects.

I feel Annie and Doc bristle at his insinuation. Gio is referring, of course, to their right to subjugate women and treat them like broodstock whenever they please. For the two females who have stood with me through everything, I turn to face Giovanni, determined not to give an inch on this subject.

"You would rather die at the hands of a mad order of humans than give the females of your pack freedom? Are there not other ways for a lycan to show loyalty that do not involve destroying their own family or forever burning away their emotions? Sacrificing females like goats is a practice that must end for the benefit of our species." I declare decisively.

"Says the sentimental fool who nearly lost his head over a pretty little fairy bi…"

This time Stefan goes too far. Before he can finish his statement, with a series of muffled pops and cracks, my par-shifted hand grabs the scrawny brat by the throat and lifts him into the air.

Don's security team bristles and moves slightly toward me, but I raise my other hand in a clear gesture of complacency.

This runt cannot even par-shift, yet he dares to mock me. I think bitterly.

"You have made it abundantly clear to me that you plan to make an enemy of this coalition solely because you resent me. So this is your final warning; provocation of violence is a direct violation of the terms set for this meeting and is punishable by immediate expulsion."

Without dropping the wriggling worm of an alpha, I turn to address the now defensive primes and their escorts.

"Can anyone here give any reasonable objection to the proposals offered in the terms of the coalition? Or are the sole objections held by this pathetic excuse for a prime and his cohorts?" I press.

Stefan's struggles grow more violent as he begins swinging his fists with the combined force of both his forms. The scrawny prime's fists connect with all the force of musket balls against my shoulder, but I have had my fair share of practice withstanding pain with a straight face.

I have to wonder; do you still think you are better than me, Stefan?

Giovanni steps forward, waving his hand in a dismissive gesture before addressing me calmly.

"I suppose there is a compromise to be had. Am I correct in assuming you would accept the implementation of combat-oriented loyalty trials on the grounds that females be given the same rights as males?"

"Assuming you afford all lycans the right to leave the pack should they find the conditions of their pack unfit. I respect all rights to enforce loyalty on those staying willingly within the pack by whatever means the alpha deems necessary under the aforementioned condition." I clarify. "Furthermore, the trade or sale of any lycanthrope without signed, uncoerced consent on the part of that lycanthrope will be strictly prohibited."

"And the punishment for non-compliance?" Gio inquires.

"You brand yourself an enemy of the coalition and if you were a signed member of the coalition then your territorial rights become stripped," I respond flatly.

With our exchange concluded and Stefan gradually running out of air, I drop the alpha like a hot potato.

For several agonizing seconds, the gathered primes of each family deliberate amongst themselves with only Australia and Africa exchanging with each other rather than keeping to themselves. As the conversations continue, Kiro can interpret who we have won over and who is still undecided or against the coalition.

With the Chinese considered neutral, how do we stack up? I inquire.

Little has changed. The Italians are against, though less so now, as are the Americans. Japan, Africa, and Australia are torn. Lots of discussions. Kiro informs me.

Not long after Kiro's assessments have been made, the deliberations end. One by one, the primes step forward to orate their decisions.

"Japan is undecidedly against."

"Italy is decidedly against."

"Russia is decidedly in favor."

"Australia is undecidedly in favor."

"America says Greyback can shove it up his…"

A low growl from the silver-haired beastkin looming behind Stefan silences him.

"Brazil is decidedly in favor."

"Africa is undecided. We simply cannot reach a decision without further discussion."

"Looks like you lose Greyback!" Stefan roars prematurely.

"Like hell he does!" A familiar voice drifts down from above as a shadow closes in over our heads.

What is she doing?

I raise my head, already fully aware of the source of the voice. Despite knowing who has intervened on my behalf, I find myself stunned. Ellesse is barely recognizable; her brilliant, outstretched wings resemble those of a monarch butterfly but stark white against thin black markings with tiny silver ivy patterns swirling between the strands of black. The underside of her majestic wingspan reminds me vividly of the night sky over her Canadian home.

More stunning than her wings are the obvious changes to her physical appearance. Since the night before last, her hair has doubled in length, roughly three inches has been added to her height, and her ivory skin is now emblazoned with shimmering green marks, as though ivy now creeps across her skin. Her regal appearance holds an eerily beautiful quality that seeps into her aura and radiates a newfound strength and confidence. If I did not know her as I do, I could easily mistake her for a goddess.

Stunning.

She certainly is. That is the fairy we always knew her to be, even if the world could not quite see it until now.

"I fail to see how a tie could be perceived as defeat." She remarks with an air of superiority as she lands lightly beside me, folding her wings with a dramatic flapping motion. She smiles at me knowingly before stepping forward to address the divided crowd herself.

"You all know Kal, and you have heard what he has to offer. However, you have yet to hear what I bring to this coalition."

"This coalition does not concern you fairy!" Stefan spits, snarling in rabid frustration.

"I, for one, would like to hear what she has to say," Jafari remarks with obvious curiosity.

With a nod, my not so little fairy continues. "As Kal has said, Don can bring you beasts and secure transport of the goods you need to protect yourselves. Kal can bring you wealth and protection through unification. *I* can bring you strength and healing like you have never known as well as the aid of the fairy race."

"The fairy race cannot help themselves, how could they, or you for that matter, bring us any power that we do not already possess?" Gio questions.

"She means to use pretty flower magic to help us!" Stefan roars with hideous laughter, earning an internal growl of contempt from Kiro, who knows firsthand how powerful Esse's *flower magic* can be.

To the surprise of everyone gathered before us, Ellesse tilts her head back and laughs in a manner truly befitting a goddess or queen. The regality of her laughter is something I have not had the privilege to witness since the last Chinese dynasty or the days of the Egyptian pharaohs.

"Yes, we certainly can do some fantastic things with plants, which you will find yourselves in need of one day if these humans are not kept in check, but that is not the advantage to be had in cooperating with my people."

Esse stretches out her hand, casting out her palm as if to throw something down upon the crowd. Then, she smiles a simple, genuine smile.

"Should you choose to align yourselves as one unified force under the laws Kal has set forth, I can offer you the power of the fullest moon, the one Kal calls the Blood Wolf Moon or Red Harvest Moon as my people call it, at any time of day."

Esse's declaration earns widened eyes and muffled gasps from the crowd who immediately begin conversing amongst themselves.

Since when can she pull off something like that? Even the omegas gifted with the moon magnification ability cannot accomplish such a task.

Since last night. Esse's chipper voice answers from within my head.

Little fairy? Is that you? Are you...speaking to me? How is this happening? I question with equal parts concern and elation.

I am not certain, but I believe this all has something to do with my blackout and the arrival of my wings. Something inside me is different...I feel, stronger.

You certainly are stronger on the outside, but I have always known you to be strong and special. This was all a long time coming if you ask me.

Moon thing? Kiro chimes in bent on staying on task despite the excitement of this newfound set of abilities.

Just sit back and see, or rather, feel, for yourself. Ellesse remarks self-assuredly.

"Doc," Ellesse speaks, silencing the crowd, "would you or Annie care to demonstrate for me?"

"S..sure," Annie responds, taken aback by Esse's sudden change in form and aura.

"What do we need to do?" Doc asks, intrigued by the turn of events.

195

"Firstly, as a healer and omega, please confirm for me that healing takes several seconds to a minute in even the youngest, strongest primes." Esse requests.

Doc nods. "I believe the fastest rate of healing I have ever observed was in an Italian heir at a rate of three seconds for a shallow knife slice that broke only a single layer of skin," Doc explains, still facing Esse.

"Could you show me your healing now?" Esse asks Annie.

"I see. Of course." Annie steps forward producing a small blade from her pocket, a tool that we all carry quite illegally. Using the blade, Annie slices a deep groove into the palm of her hand breaking the first two layers of skin. The wound bleeds for several seconds, then heals.

Ellesse holds out one hand, palm turned upward, then turns to Doc.

"Wipe her hand clean then try that again." She instructs.

The two females do as they are instructed. However, when Annie slices her hand open this time, the blade manages only to sever the top layer of skin for the briefest fraction of a second, healing before it can produce any blood.

"Incredible!" Doc exclaims, rushing forward to examine the results. "You used the same amount of force?" She questions Annie excitedly.

"Yes…this is remarkable. I did not feel a thing. Not even a pin-prick of pain!" Annie laughs in gleeful excitement at this newfound ability.

"This is a cheap trick!" Stefan objects, his voice breaking ever so slightly under the strain of knowing he has lost. The veins in the young alpha's forehead protrude, revealing his truly volatile nature.

"Then test it for yourself, unless, of course, you are too afraid to see the result." I shrug casually, doing all that I can to hide my overwhelming excitement at Esse's wondrous abilities.

Not one to be put down, Stefan rips a chunk of flesh from his arm using his jaws. The gesture, meant to be a dramatic display of strength, falls flat as the tissue visible reforms before the eyes of the onlooking lycans. Within three brief seconds, the wound ceases to exist with only a tiny circle of blood, no bigger than a quarter, having been spilled.

"Well. I, for one, am sold."

That voice...I know that voice.

A shadowy figure, flanked by two equally lithe shadows, appears in the doorway escorted by two of the beast-kin guards.

"Don said I could find you all here. Sorry, my invite came a bit late, and I have been a very busy lady. However, I have not come empty-handed; China is decidedly in favor of the proposed coalition. So says the newly named prime alpha; Jade Fong."

The mysterious figure throws off her cloak, boasting a proud smile. Her two companions follow suit. The three females standing before me are easily recognizable by scent as Chinese lycans belonging to the coastal region of the territory. In a bizarre twist of fate, the female standing at the center of the trio is none other than my old acquaintance, Jade.

You know her? Esse asks within my mind.

Yes. You do too, from my stories.

The Jade? The one you never saw again after she supposedly sailed away to freedom! Esse questions excitedly.

The very same. Kiro confirms.

"Jade! I see your life of freedom has done wonders for you. Did I hear correctly; do you mean to say that you now preside over the Chinese prime's territory as head of their pack? How did such a series of events come to pass?"

"A long story indeed. Don wrote a letter for you explaining it all but for this meeting, I will paraphrase. My father, who is also the father of Feng, the deposed criminal, is dead. Feng, as fate would have it, killed him in a fit of rage. That is why the welp fled. He feared retaliation from his brothers. Unbeknownst to my dear brothers, I have been very much alive for all this time just waiting for the old man to bite it. When he did, I seized control from my inexperienced, and fairly pampered, brothers and now stand before you as the victorious and recognized prime alpha of China." Jade explains.

"And the last name Fong?" I pry.

"He still has not learned to leave well enough alone." This time it is the companion to Jade's right that answers my inquiry.

"How rude of me. May I introduce to you, old friend, my partner, and right hand, Lin Fong. There is so much irony to be had in our meeting." Jade remarks lightheartedly.

"Enough!" Stefan roars, the veins in his forehead protruding more than ever. "This will not stand. This bitch cannot be a prime alpha."

"The Russians recognize Jade's ascension to the role of prime alpha and her claim to the territory of China," Ivan remarks casually before Stefan can take his rant any farther.

"The Brazilians second that recognition," Carlos adds.

"I too recognize Jade's claim," I remark smugly, making three official witnesses to Jade's claim.

Jafari steps forward flanked by the Japanese prime alpha.

"Africa is now decidedly in favor of the proposed coalition."

"Japan is now also decidedly in favor."

"There you have it, everyone! A momentous occasion indeed! Not only does the coalition move forward along with the first stage of our plan to rid the world of the influence of the wicked Order, but we do so with our first female prime alpha among our ranks!" I announce, not bothering to hold back my excitement at this astonishing turn of events.

Who would have thought three hundred years of work would end like this. I wonder to myself in awe. *All that we have lost and all those who are no longer with us to see this day through. . .I have finally done right by them. Perhaps it was all worth it in the end.*

I give a wave of my hand and a slight bow to Jade, indicating that she should be the first to sign her name to the document sprawled out across the table in the front of the room, just before the platform.

A grisly sound interrupts Jade's approach. We both turn to witness a fully enraged Stefan attempting to unify the two primary lycanthrope forms into one.

"Stefan! Stop this at once! The rules of the gathering are clear; would you dare to break tradition before all the primes? By continually challenging me you have already made yourself an enemy to this coalition, do not make matters worse by attacking others in a peaceful gathering on neutral ground." I caution, wanting nothing more than to avoid sullying this momentous occasion with the spilling of more blood.

Stefan opens his mouth, no doubt to utter some sarcastic retort, but his vocals have already merged and are now caught somewhere between those of a wolf and a man. These twisted vocals produce a guttural screech that threatens to shatter the sensitive ears of all in the room, Ellesse most of all. Her delicate fairy ears are as sensitive as those of a bat and pick up the jumbled frequencies with a resounding echo.

I can feel the piercing needles of pain erupting in her head as if they were my own. Rage flows through me as I lock eyes with the beast that was formerly Stefan, an eternal thorn in my side. His eyes now flicker between the blue-green eyes of his human self and the deep brown eyes of his rabid wolf, a notoriously brutal creature with no sense of compassion and very limited emotional range. Caught in this suspended state, Stefan no longer forms reasoned thoughts, his actions are driven by impulse alone as he and his wolf both vie for control over their hideously combined bodies.

Jade steps forward to intervene but her path is barred by Carlos and Ivan.

"This is a matter that he must face alone if he is to serve as this coalition's guardian," Carlos informs a fuming Jade.

"That is utter bullshit." Jade huffs indignantly. She turns toward Esse seeking a more level head. "Can you stand there and say that these traditions are acceptable to you? Will you let their outdated rules put him in danger?"

For a moment I fear that Esse will side with Jade. Instead, she calmly steps forward, flexing her awe-inspiring wings, and addresses Jade as though she were a childhood friend.

"Of course I am not content to let tradition put Kal or anyone else in harm's way. I know what blindly following traditions can cost, but this is something Kal needs to face. Moreover, I know this is something he can face. Believe me, Kal is not, nor will he ever be, alone. That is the point in forming this coalition; the era of every creature for themselves is dead and gone. Such outdated sentiments end here. I am choosing to stand aside and put my faith in Kal, because I know he feels the same way I do, and I know that he is strong enough to prevail."

Esse then turns to address the monstrosity that is rapidly losing control of its functions.

"Kal has told me a bit about this form you have taken. If you can even understand me now through your blind rage and unbridled hatred, then know this: sacrificing your body and mind to challenge Kal personally, knowing all the while that you have lost, will lead only to your death. I hope for the sake of all lycan kind, and no doubt the world as a whole, that the violence will end here."

With that, my profoundly wise fairy steps back, putting her faith in me as she has always has.

Words cannot express how touched I am that Esse would place her trust in me. I can only hope that I have the strength to live up to her expectations.

"Stefan, we have had our differences, but your story does not need to end this way. Disentangle your forms now and we can discuss this like levelheaded adults."

My words come too late for Stefan, not that they would have done any good had they been spoken sooner. The now fully enraged monstrosity, formerly known as Stefan, whirls, and snaps violently at the closest lycans. Fortunately, his fused form is all brawn and not much else; the hideous double muscling of his carelessly hybridized legs slows the beast down, making for easily dodged attacks. His simplistically formed mind makes for predictable movements as well.

"Stefan!" I call out to the monster before me, drawing its attention to something I know it cannot resist; me.

The maddened mongrel turns with a slow growl and charges me instantly, giving no thought to its actions. Chairs and fragments of tables and carpet go flying as Stefan's oversized body and claws move through the narrow aisle of the meeting hall like a spiked wrecking ball.

In a single, anticlimactic motion I bring an end to Stefan's rage forever. With an effortlessness that comes only from centuries of practice, I throw the combined strength of Kiro and myself into my left arm and wrist while par-shifting the right as I have practiced hundreds of times.

As Stefan's disfigured jaws snap shut around my left forearm, I rip a precise hole into his chest with my par-shifted hand, clawing out his heart in a single stroke with pinpoint accuracy.

Not cleaning it up. Kiro asserts.

Stefan's jaws release my arm, and his beastly form utters one final shriek before falling to the ground dead.

A stunned silence falls over the gathered crowd, as all eyes flicker from Stefan's corpse to me.

"*This* is what the old ways get you." I declare, holding the heart of the fallen prime aloft for emphasis.

"Whether the executioner is me protecting the coalition I have worked so hard to establish, or the Order picking off those who fail to accept the coalition's protection, death will come to all who are too stubborn to progress. Anyone who wishes to stand against our unification as a species shall be felled as easily as a tree in a storm. The days of fighting, killing, and selling one another are over. As punishment for his shortcomings as an alpha, Stefan's territories shall be divided as they would have had he ascended during the reign of the coalition. Canada will now become its separate territory and an alpha of the coalition's approved choice shall be appointed to it. I believe we are finished here."

"To clarify, as a representative of the fairy race, I recognize the authority of this coalition and agree to grant any aid necessary only to recognized members of the aforementioned coalition of primes." Esse restates.

One by one, each prime alpha steps forward to offer their signature, with the American's being permitted one week to decide on a new prime alpha to lead them, at which point a Canadian alpha will be chosen from among the packs already living within the established territory. As I watch my entire life's work realized before my eyes, I feel an unexpected emptiness.

This is what we wanted. Kiro reminds me, though even he sounds uncertain now.

Is it? We just killed someone who opposed us to make a point and protect our cause. How is what we did any different than what Feng was trying to do or what our ancestors did to our parents or even what the Order is doing?

We are not them! Kiro declares defensively.

The Order believes what they are doing to be right. Who is to say they are not right? What is right and what is wrong is decided by the victor and the masses. Has what we have done been worth the outcome? I muse.

We cannot afford to dwell on that now. Worth it or not, we are here and the members of two species are now counting on us. We will make the outcome worth the blood. Kiro assures me with a surprising level of optimism.

At least we will not be facing the next phase of our journey alone.

Were neither of you listening to my grand speech? Esse chimes in. *You were never alone.*

Some months later.

"Why are we out here in the snow again?" Annie asks through her com, carefully situated in her tree perch nearly a kilometer away.

"We have been over this. As the head of the coalition..."

"You mean Kal'ban," Annie interjects in her most sing-song voice.

"If you insist on calling me that, fine, but that is your name for me, not mine." I resist the urge to grin at Annie's newfound cheerful side. "The youngest male heir to the Dracul family line contacted me with a request to enter our territory. Well, more precisely, an old friend contacted me on the heir's behalf."

"There you go being vague again. You are turning into Red by the day." Esse laughs as she lands lightly beside me.

As the months have passed her wings have only become more brilliant and her inherent connection to nature has reached new heights. The very world around us, and every living thing within it, seem determined to protect her at any cost.

"That tends to happen when one is as chronically tired as I am. We cannot all be blessed with your boundless energy, my fairy." I remind her with a friendly smile.

"Some details would be nice." Annie urges.

"You ladies sure hate surprises. You will see who we are meeting soon enough. All you need to know is that my contact is a creature with certain...interesting tastes."

"That does not sound ominous at all." Esse pouts teasingly.

"Esse, you said you wanted to learn more about the other non-human factions. I have taught you, in the last few months, about the ghouls and shifters who run the underground networks that keep our existence hidden from the human masses. I have even taught you about the species from which we lycanthropes were born, the beast-kin. Now it is time for you to learn about one more very famous and very important faction. This next species is responsible for protecting non-humans living within the heart of human societies, especially major cities, in exchange for the rest of us non-humans providing them with food during times of need."

"Food?" Esse inquires suspiciously. "What do these non-humans eat?"

"Sorry to interrupt the lesson, but you are about to find out Ellesse," Annie remarks, knowing better than Esse who the Dracul family is and what faction they fall into.

Sure enough, Annie's eyes are as sharp as ever. Approaching with blinding speed is a group of six non-humans.

"I see the rumors are true. Your daylight susceptibility does intensify with age." I remark casually, knowing that the approaching group will hear me without fail.

"You have clearly gotten a big head already, old friend." A tall, broad-shouldered man with black hair and dark eyes approaches me with a welcome expression.

"Good to see you, Edgar," I remark pleasantly, grinning to myself.

"This must be the fairy we have heard so much about. I wish we had time to discuss joining your most recent endeavor, but we are in quite a hurry."

"So I gather. I wish I could speed things along more but, per protocol, I need to know your business here. We have taken on more heat from the Order than we need as it is. I am sure you understand."

"We do not have time for this." A lean but well-muscled male with golden-brown eyes and shoulder-length dark hair steps forward. An agitated look creases every feature of his attractive face and his aura emanates a cold defensiveness.

"I apologize on behalf of my companion. This matter is personal for him. We...have lost some of our own. Too many of our own, in fact." Edgar apologizes solemnly.

"Believe me, I understand. We will accommodate you." I turn my attention to Esse.

"Ellesse, meet Drago, the grandson of the fabled Dracula and heir to the kingdom of the vampiric faction."